ENDORS

"JC KNOWS HOW TO WEAVE A TALE THAT KEEPS YOU ON THE EDGE OF YOUR SEAT AND WANTING MORE EVEN AFTER YOU'VE FINISHED THE LAST PAGE."
~ DRINKFROMTHEETERNALWELL.BLOGSPOT.COM

"THIS BOOK WAS BREATHTAKINGLY BEAUTIFUL."
~ KASFIRE REVIEWS

"DROP EVERYTHING YOU'RE DOING AND READ IT. RIGHT NOW. IF YOU LIKE YA, ROMANCE, EDGE-OF-YOUR-SEAT SUSPENSE, READ. THIS. BOOK."
~ MICHELE HARPER, AUTHOR OF THE YA SERIES *WISDOM AND FOLLY*

"ONE OF MY FAVORITE THINGS ABOUT THIS AUTHOR IS THAT HER STORYTELLING IS DIFFERENT, FULL OF HEART, AND PURE."
~ KARA GRANT,

"JC MORROWS HAS AN AMAZING TALENT FOR WRITING SPECULATIVE FICTION. ENGAGING AND FULL OF SUSPENSE, HER WORK KEEPS ME ON THE EDGE OF MY SEAT . . . FROM THE FIRST PARAGRAPH, I FOUND MYSELF UNABLE TO PUT DOWN THE STORY UNTIL THE VERY LAST WORD."
~ NAOMI MILLER, AMAZON BEST-SELLING AUTHOR

"THE WORDPLAY AND CHARACTERS DREW ME IN FROM THE START. I CAN'T WAIT TO CONTINUE READING THE SERIES."
~ BOOKWORM LISA REVIEWS

"PERFECT FOR FANS THAT LOVE A GOOD LOVE STORY IN THE BACKGROUND OF A HIGH FANTASY UNIVERSE."
~ BOOK BRIEFS REVIEWS

"ONCE AGAIN, JC MORROWS HAS GRIPPED ME WITH HER WORDS. THE SKILL IN WHICH SHE PAIRS WORDS TOGETHER TO CREATE AN ALTERNATE WORLD IS NOTHING SHORT OF AMAZING."
~ *TONI SHILOH, AUTHOR OF THE MAPLE RUN SERIES*

"AN EXTREMELY WELL WRITTEN BOOK WITH A CONSISTENT, ALMOST BREATHLESS PACE. YOU WILL FIND YOURSELF COMPLETELY IMMERSED IN THIS. MOVE OVER HUNGER GAMES, A NEW CHALLENGER HAS ARRIVED ON THE SCENE!"

~READERS FAVORITE

"JC MORROWS BUILDS SUSPENSE AND AN OMINOUS SETTING THAT WILL LEAVE YOU EAGER TO READ MORE."

~ A. J. CATTAPAN - AUTHOR OF THE YA NOVEL ANGELHOOD

"THE AUTHOR WRITES AN ACTION PACKED STORY THAT WILL KEEP YOU ON THE EDGE OF YOUR SEAT TRYING TO READ FASTER AND TURN THE PAGES FASTER TO SEE WHAT IS GOING TO HAPPEN NEXT."

~ GOODREADS

"FULL OF ACTION, SUSPENSE AND A WORLD TURNED COLD!"

~ GOODREADS

"THIS IS A TRUE DYSTOPIAN FANTASY NOVEL, BUT IT HAS ITS OWN UNIQUENESS RATHER THAN RIDING THE COAT TAILS OF PREVIOUS WORKS, AS SO MANY SEEM TO DO."

~MISSICA SKEENS PULLEN

"LIFE AFTER E.L.E. PROVIDED ALL THE ELEMENTS TO KEEP ME INTERESTED THROUGHOUT DECEMBER. MY EVENINGS WERE FILLED WITH ACTION, SUSPENSE, AND ROMANCE."

~ JANNETTE FULLER

"JC MORROWS GRABS YOUR ATTENTION ON THE FIRST PAGE AND DOESN'T LET GO UNTIL YOU COME TO THE END. ALL HER BOOKS LEAVE YOU WANTING AND READY TO READ THE NEXT IN THE SERIES. ENJOY!"

~ TONI SHILOH, AUTHOR OF AN UNLIKELY PROPOSAL

"LIFE AFTER E.L.E. IS A POST APOCALYPTIC DYSTOPIAN THAT WILL KEEP YOU TURNING THE PAGES. J.C. MORROWS IS A MUST-READ AUTHOR!"

~ MANDY FENDER, AWARD WINNING AUTHOR OF THE DEFIER SERIES

"LIFE AFTER E.L.E. LEFT ME DUMBSTRUCK . . . AND HAPPY AND SAD AND EXCITED AND WEEPY AND A LITTLE BIT IN LOVE. IT'S VERY HUNGER GAMES MEETS THE DAY AFTER TOMORROW. IF YOU ARE LOOKING FOR AN EXCITING FAST-PACED READ, THIS IS THE STORY FOR YOU!"

~ Julie Hall, USA Today Bestselling Author

ON *THE ORDER OF THE MOONSTONE SERIES*

"THE ORDER OF THE MOONSTONE SERIES HAS THE POTENTIAL OF BEING A FAN FAVORITE."

~ MUGGLENET, THE WORLD'S #1 *HARRY POTTER* SITE

"I WAS INTRIGUED BEFORE I EVEN STARTED READING BECAUSE OF THE KILLER PREMISE *(NO PUN INTENDED)* . . ."

~ LYDIA THOMAS, AUTHOR OF *THE FIELD*

"THE ORDER OF THE MOONSTONE SERIES IS A MUST READ FOR ANYONE INTO DYSTOPIAN FICTION. *HUNGER GAMES* FANS WILL LOVE IT—OR, AT LEAST THIS ONE DOES."

~ NICOLE L RIVERA, AUTHOR OF *FINDING UNAUTHORIZED FAITH IN HARRY POTTER*

"THE ORDER OF THE MOONSTONE SERIES IS FILLED WITH PLENTY OF ROMANTIC TENSION, INTRIGUE, AND SUSPENSE."

~ MARISSA SHROCK, AUTHOR OF *THE FIRST PRINCIPLE*

"AN EXPLOSION OF INTRIGUE AND KEEPS YOU MESMERIZED BY THE AUTHOR'S GIFT FOR BEAUTIFULLY WRITTEN WORDS THAT COME TO LIFE."

~ TEXAS BOOK-AHOLIC

"JC MORROWS IS SUCH A TALENTED WRITER . . . WHO ELSE LOVES HER READERS SO MUCH THAT SHE WOULD WRITE A SHORT STORY OF THINGS HAPPENING IN A BOOK THAT'S ALREADY BEEN RELEASED!"

~ GOODREADS REVIEWER

BOOKS BY JC

WITH MACY MORROWS

~ TALES OF A TEENAGE ALIEN HUMAN HYBRID ~

The Alien's Daughter
The Hybrid Challenge
The Human Complication
COMING SOON

~ SILVER CITY PRINCESS STORIES ~

Cindy's Demanding Day
A Challenge for Maree
Rissa's Secret Recipe
Isabelle and the Beastly Bookworm
COMING SOON

Siren's CHARM

CALL OF THE SEA · BOOK ONE

Siren's Charm

CALL OF THE SEA · BOOK ONE

JC MORROWS

*Bestselling author of **A Reluctant Assassin***

Siren's Charm
Copyright © 2019 JC Morrows

Mystic Moonstone Press: an imprint of S&G Publishing, Knoxville, TN
www.mysticmoonstonepress.wordpress.com

Morrows, JC

  Siren's Charm / JC Morrows

1. Fiction / Sirens and Sea Monsters. 2. Fiction / Mermaids. 3. Fiction / Adventure. 4. Fiction / Urban Fantasy. 5. Fiction / Science Fiction & Fantasy / Supernatural. 6. Fiction / Science Fiction & Fantasy

ISBN: 978-1948733243 HARDBOUND
ISBN: 978-1948733250 PAPERBACK

Cover and Internal Design © 2024 Expresso Designs
Cover Image by Expresso Designs

First Edition 2024

PRINTED AND BOUND IN THE UNITED STATES OF AMERICA

for Macy,
who has always wanted
to be a mermaid.

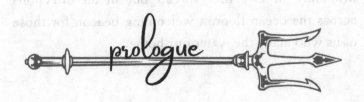

prologue

FLOATING EFFORTLESSLY IN THE water, the warmth of the sun soaking into my skin, I trailed a hand over the water's surface, tiny waves lapping at my fingers as they trailed back and forth in the cool water.

Someone swam past, splashing, but I didn't open my eyes. Someone else shouted from the far end of the pool. Still I kept my eyes closed. I just lay there, floating, all the while letting my imagination carry me away, tuning out the sounds of my brother and cousins as they ran and played and splashed all around me.

In my mind, I wasn't floating on the surface of the water. I was swimming along underneath the water, propelled forward by an enormous tail covered in shimmery scales in a thousand shades of purple and pink and silver, swimming along in a crowd who were all heading in the same direction, toward an impressive pearl white castle at the center of a brilliantly lit city that spread out in all directions across the ocean floor, a welcoming beacon for those of us who made the water our home.

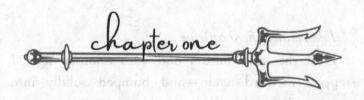

LOOKING DOWN AT MY PHONE AS I WALKED through the store, I purposely slowed my steps as I answered the message that appeared.

Let me know when you get there.

Then, before I could type more than a word. . .

Be sure to check on all three.
And ask about any sort of deals they have going.
Find out if they match prices.

3

My breath whooshed out as I typed as fast as possible on the tiny little screen, trying to answer all of the questions quickly, so I could get the errand over with and visit my favorite coffee place.

I'm almost there. I will. Yes. OK.

I desperately need caffeine.

I hit the send button and with another sigh, I stepped forward again—and bumped solidly into someone. When I looked up at him, it was easy to see that he had been standing right in front of me the whole time. I just hadn't seen him. Embarrassment sent heat rushing into my cheeks, likely turning them a bright shade of red.

Oh my word. How did I miss seeing him there?

Even as the thought came to me, I knew the answer. I had been staring at my phone.

Feeling ridiculous, fumbling in my mind for some way to apologize, I just stood there, staring up at him. It was difficult to look away. Especially since he was well over six feet tall, broad-shouldered, and clearly well-muscled. Bumping into him had felt like ramming into a wall.

And standing there. . . just looking at him, the strangest thing happened. I completely and totally lost track of time. I mean, it could have been a second—or an hour—but there was literally no way to know how long I stood there, just staring at him.

At some point, the heat of embarrassment changed into a different type of heat. Everything about him, from his dark, wavy hair to his tall, muscular physique, to his well tailored clothes, told me this man was about as far out of my league as you could get.

At that point, I forcibly stopped myself from staring. I made myself look down, finally finding my voice and mumbling something that I dearly hoped sounded like an apology.

"Not at all, Miss. Please excuse me." The deep, masculine voice sent a little shiver along my skin, almost as if the man had brushed a kiss along my neck instead of the whisper of breath that had reached me with his words.

"Oh, no. . . I. . ." I made the mistake of looking up at him again and words failed me. It was not something I was accustomed to—having been teased my entire life about my ability to strike up a conversation with a perfect stranger and know their entire life story in the course of a long line waiting to order coffee. But no words came now. Not to me, anyway.

"Are you all right?" Again, his voice sent a little shiver along my skin and I could only nod, struck dumb by my disorienting reaction to him.

"Are you certain?" He asked the question as his eyes searched my face and beyond—presumably for outward signs of an injury.

When he took my hand a moment later and led me

over to where mattresses were lined up side by side in long rows, the heat that had started to build in my midsection spread to my arm. . . and every square inch in between. Everywhere his hand touched mine, it felt as if it were aflame and I began to wonder if I had done some sort of damage, though I didn't remember hitting my head—and surely that was the only thing that would account for such confusion and ridiculous behavior.

"I. . ." None of the words I wanted to say would form on my tongue, and I shook my head in an attempt to clear it.

My phone chose that moment to vibrate, and when he dropped my hand, the fuzzy thoughts in my head started to clear a bit. I looked down at my mother's message with a sense of relief.

She might have been annoying me before, but she was saving me now—and I would not forget it anytime soon.

Are you there yet?

I typed in a quick reply.

Yes. I just got here.

Then I took a deep breath, almost hoping that when I looked up again, the strange, oddly compelling man would be gone. But he was still standing beside me, looking down at my phone with an odd expression on his handsome features.

Now the words came, flooding out and tumbling over each other on their rush out of my mouth.

"Sorry. She's just really concerned over this mattress. She saw they were on sale, and I just happened to be out, so she sent me to check out the situation. It's been way too long since we replaced ours, so we really need new ones." The moment the words left my mouth, I realized what I had just said to this stranger who I had essentially run into only moments before—and the heat rushed back to my cheeks.

Fortunately, he was either a gentleman or somehow he hadn't picked up on my major *faux-pas*. "Well, I suppose I should let you get on with it, then." He stepped back a little, then stopped. "If you're certain you are all right. . . ."

"I am. Thank you." He nodded and moved away. I stayed right where I was for a few more seconds, desperately trying to slow my erratic heartbeat.

When I stood, I walked aimlessly around the area, trying to make it look as if I were shopping, but nothing I was looking at made any sense to my muddled brain. There were too many thoughts rushing around to make sense of even one of them. Nothing made sense in my head. My reaction to him had been completely unexpected—and intense in a way I was not used to.

There was still a ridiculous amount of heat on my cheeks, my arm, my chest. There was also a tingle lingering on my skin where he had touched me. My breathing had not yet returned to normal and for some strange reason, I felt a strong urge to giggle.

This is ridiculous. I told myself. *Why am I feeling like a teenager—at my age? I feel like this is a dream, but if it's a dream I wouldn't know it. Would I?*

I had never really been one to giggle over boys and make a fool of myself, so my behavior felt doubly odd. Clearly, it had been too long since I had been around a handsome man. I pinched my arm to be sure I wasn't dreaming.

Ouch! Not dreaming. So he was real. Whoa! He certainly was unexpected. I don't know when I've met a more handsome man.

My blood felt as if it was rushing everywhere. My heartbeat was still erratic. My breaths were still coming a little too fast. When had a good looking man ever affected me this way?

Since I couldn't think of a time, I decided to go back to the idea that I had somehow smacked my head—either when I'd bumped into him or just after.

Maybe on a shelf when I stumbled backwards—and that's why everything still feels a little confused and muddled in my head...

Indeed, it did. The more I tried to focus on what exactly had happened when I'd bumped into him, the less clear it was in my head.

8

So I stopped trying. Obviously it wasn't helping.

The notification sound from my phone reminded me what I was supposed to be doing. I shook myself a little and tried to focus on the task at hand; finding those mattresses. Looking around me, still trying to clear the confusion in my head, I realized I had stopped in front of one of the three mattresses Mom had actually sent me to look at. Laughing at myself a little now—*I mean, just how ridiculous is this day going to get*—I tried to focus, to really look at the information on the sign next to it.

Everything was just like I had expected it to be, which was good since I was still feeling a little loopy and silly. Using my phone, I took a picture of the sign, glad to have an easy out, before looking around again to see if I could spot one of the others.

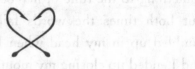

When I left the store, I intended to drive straight to my favorite coffee shop. However, my head still felt like it was spinning, and I took two wrong turns before actually arriving there.

Once I did, I sat in my car for nearly a minute, still trying to get my heart to calm down. Just the tiniest thought of the man I'd encountered would send it racing, dragging my breath with it, leaving me feeling loopy and light-headed and almost as if I weren't even touching the ground around me.

Caffeine. That's what I need. Something to wake me up, snap me out of this. Two wrong turns! I'm surprised I even made it to the coffee shop.

Squaring my shoulders, I stepped out of the car, closed the door, turned toward the store, and nearly tripped over my own feet.

Standing there, right by the door, was the same man I was trying desperately to get out of my head. Well, to be honest, I kept thinking about him, so I wasn't trying very hard.

Why? Why is he here? How is that possible?

I tried twice to open my mouth and make some sort of flippant remark about what a small world it was or something to the tune of maybe he was following me, but both times the words failed me. They got all jumbled up in my head when I started to say them, and I ended up closing my mouth again.

He didn't move until I got close to the door. I couldn't tell if he was simply being a gentleman, waiting to open the door for me or if he actually was waiting for me. I moved slowly, doing my best to keep any part of my body from touching him.

Just to be safe.

I did not want or need my brain getting jumbled again, and some part of me was pretty certain I would have the same reaction if I even brushed up against him. Fortunately, I made it through the door and into the coffee shop without touching any part of him. However, he walked through the doorway right behind me, so closely that I could almost swear I could feel heat from his body.

I made my way to the line. And he followed me all the way. I stepped up behind an older lady who looked as if she had no idea what she wanted or how to figure it out.

Normally, I would have struck up a conversation with her, made a joke or a silly comment about how many choices they gave us, but I was having more difficulty than I wanted to admit making sense of the menu myself. I often made a point of trying new things, but I couldn't seem to decide what I was in the mood for.

Fortunately, the barista behind the counter recognized me when I stepped up. "Your usual today or are you trying something new?"

I looked up at the menu again, still trying to make sense of it, but after a few seconds, I knew it was hopeless so I caved. "Make it the usual."

"The usual it is, then. And I'm going to add a shot of coffee. You look like you need it today." She spoke quietly, but I could see concern in her eyes.

She knew me pretty well, had seen me on some of my craziest days—the sort of days I would joke about needing my coffee in an IV drip. If she thought I looked like I needed a jolt of something, I must be worse off than I was thinking.

Unsure of what to say—and more than a little worried about what might come out, especially with the handsome stranger still right behind me—I nodded my head, waved my phone over the little sensor to pay and then moved away.

When I stepped to the side, I did not anticipate the distance well enough, or else he had moved closer to me. I bumped solidly into him again and every thought in my head turned to mush—again. It felt... delicious.

All I could do was stand there and let the feeling surround me... first, the heat that felt as if it were pouring out of him and into me, then the confusion as my thoughts scattered every which way in my head. The heat of embarrassment was filling my cheeks— again. And there was a strange feeling underneath it all, something that I couldn't quite latch onto, even though it felt as if it were pulling at me, dragging at me, trying to move my whole being—somehow.

It almost felt as if he were trying to communicate with me, as if there was a tiny little voice inside, telling me something... but what, I had no idea. And how... I had no idea how, either.

Suddenly the heat cooled just a little. It didn't disappear entirely, but it did give me enough room in my head to step away. Nearly everything within me wanted to turn and look at him again as I moved toward the door, but the tiniest part of me knew that would be a very bad idea—and though, it was likely the most difficult thing I had ever done, I slowly walked over to where I would pick up my coffee.

Not more than a minute later, he walked up beside me, obviously waiting as well. It took every ounce of self control I could get hold of to keep myself from looking up at him. We stood there for about a minute before my name was called. I picked up my drink and turned away from the counter as quickly as possible, nearly colliding with a young woman who had come up behind me to wait for her own order.

Once I sidestepped her, I rushed toward the door. I nearly turned back around when I saw that he was standing right there, waiting to open it for me again. It was several seconds before I could get my feet to move.

He just stood there, with a sort of half smile on his ridiculously handsome features, waiting—for me, obviously.

I was careful again to avoid touching or brushing against him, but the heat I'd felt before was there, almost as if it were reaching out to me and I could feel my breathing speed up. My heart started pounding, and my thoughts scattered again.

What is wrong with me? What is it about this man? Why can't I seem to shake this off?

But there was no answer—none at all. I pushed myself to move quickly through the doorway and head for my car, not daring to look back at him or see which direction he went.

I should have... and I would have... if only I could have.

But again my thoughts were muddled. About two seconds after I shut my door, I turned to set down my coffee, and let out a yelp when I saw him sitting in my passenger seat.

"What are you doing?" I half yelled, half whispered the question, worried first that I might elicit some strange reaction in him, second that someone outside the car might see or hear me and get a wrong impression of what was going on.

"I'm here for you." That deep, masculine, slightly husky voice danced along every nerve in my body, again sending chills and shivers up and down my spine even while visions of dark rooms and late nights, steamy encounters and passionate embraces filled my head.

He wasn't touching any part of me, but my body felt as if he were running his hands all over me. It was a sensation I was not accustomed to. I wanted to demand he get out of my car. I wanted to beg him to stay. I wanted to ask him what he meant. I wanted to move across the seat and climb into his lap.

The last thought shocked me more than a little — actually, quite a lot. Where had that come from? I didn't think things like that — normally. It must be something he was doing. Somehow. I wanted to blame him for doing something to me, while I was desperate to enjoy whatever was happening to me.

Was there some control he had over me that I was not aware of? There was no other explanation that made any sense. As if any of the things that had happened since the moment I first bumped into him made even a tiny amount of sense.

Just when panic started to take hold of me, I told myself to lean back, take a deep breath, then look at him with some sort of detachment. However, he didn't give me the chance. He leaned forward, slid a hand into my hair and covered my lips with his.

The heat that had been running through me ever since I'd first collided with him exploded when his lips touched mine. Every thought I'd started to collect, every question, every fear, every worry... every one of them scattered into tiny little shards of nothing and I felt myself lean into the kiss, unexpectedly hungry for more. Much more.

All on its own, my hand moved up his jacket and wrapped around his neck. I tilted my head a little as his lips moved over mine. That same heat wrapped itself in little tendrils around every part of me until I felt like I was a flame being consumed by an unexplainable force that held me to him like a lifeline.

His other hand moved around to my back, pulling me even closer to him while he deepened the kiss. My mouth opened on a soft moan as his lips moved away from my mouth, but any complaint I might have had drifted away as his lips scorched a path down my neck and across my collarbone.

He said something against my skin, but nothing registered in my brain outside of the heat and passion crashing over me in strong, intense waves. I tried to pay attention when he spoke again, but nothing he was saying made a bit of sense. I shook my head a little when he pulled away. and he looked at me with a somewhat odd expression on his face.

And then those waves crashing over me felt real. Suddenly I was cold—icy cold. In shock, I sputtered, trying to wiggle out of his grip, to move away from him, to catch my breath in the suffocating vortex of cold that was pulling me under.

And then everything went black.

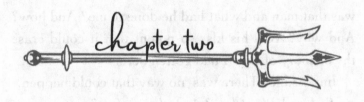

chapter two

I WOKE SCREAMING, CATAPULTING myself upright as I opened my eyes to an unfamiliar room filled with a strange light. It took no more than that to tell me I had no idea where I was so it seemed likely that I did not belong here.

I looked around at the furniture that looked as if it belonged to another century, and the obviously expensive light fixture—even though it did not appear to be an actual source of light. And I was even more confused. How had I gotten here. . . when. . . who had brought me. . . and why?

What happened to me? Did I faint?

I tried to think through my day... tried to think

back to what I remembered happening last. Suddenly, without warning, heat flooded through me as the feel of *his* lips on mine filled my head. I remembered the heat, the tingling, the scattered thoughts. Was that why I was having so much difficulty remembering what had happened to me, because of that kiss? Who was that man and what had he done to me? And how? And why? Was his kiss so potent that it could erase the memory of how I had gotten here.

Impossible! There was no way that could happen.

So how did I get here? And where is here?

There was no one in the room with me, but there was a closed door directly in front of me. I couldn't help but wonder if there was someone on the other side of it who could tell me what was going on, where I was, and how I had gotten there.

I opened my mouth to call out, but something stopped me. Panic suddenly flared within me. What if anyone on the other side of the door was with him — working with him? Or for him? Would they answer my questions? Would they even open the door? Or would they just leave me in this room with no answers and worries piling on top of one another?

It was maddening not to know... not to remember... to be in a strange place with no idea how I had gotten there or why. Somehow I felt pretty certain that the man who had been following me had done this to me.

What was his deal? What was his game? And how was I going to find out — without being manipulated by him even more? That question frightened me more than anything else.

Clearly he had some sort of power over me. It could be drugs. I had watched enough cop shows to know that when a woman did something she really didn't want to do around a man, drugs were usually at the bottom of it all.

And he was obviously much stronger than me. He had brought me here, unconscious—or at least heavily drugged since I had no memory of it. So how was I going to do anything? How was I supposed to get out of this mess?

I looked around slowly, trying to shake off the fog that had filled my head since I woke up. I needed to find something familiar in the room, something that might help me figure out what had happened or how I had gotten there.

All I could think of was that kiss. When I tried to think of what had happened afterwards, every memory seemed foggy, unclear, scattered.

Did I hit my head—again?

Was that why I had felt as if I was being pulled under? Was that what it was like to black out? The feeling of blackness pulling at me was suddenly so overwhelming, I couldn't catch my breath.

Drugs. It must be drugs someone gave me.

The thought both frightened me and reassured me. That had to be the explanation then. The psycho man had drugged me. Maybe when I bumped into him.

There must have been something on his jacket that transferred through skin.

But had my bare skin brushed his jacket — or had my sleeve?

Did they make drugs that would transfer through fabric? Wouldn't that mean it would have affected him, too? Wouldn't he have been just as dazed and out of it as me? Maybe he had been inoculated in some way against the effects. Or maybe he had built up some superhuman tolerance to them. Maybe he had done this so many times, they had no effect on him after all this time.

Who is this guy?

Again, images of women being abducted and men selling them to the highest bidder flashed through my brain. I shook my head at the runaway train my thoughts had gotten onto.

Ok. Stop it! Obviously I've watched too many TV shows...

There had to be a logical explanation to all of this. And there would also be some sort of logical way to get out of it. I just had to find it.

With that in mind, I decided the best thing to do would be to open the door and hope there was someone on the other side who could... and would... answer my questions.

So, I pushed my way off of the bed — and I found myself floating... I couldn't really see water around me, but if I were floating there had to be water — or something — all around me.

But wait. That's impossible. Isn't it?

I moved again. Nope. Impossible or not, I floated off the bed. Moving my arms a bit, I managed to move into somewhat of an upright position. And then the panic was back, trying to choke me.

How am I floating? Am I underwater? I can't be in space?

I couldn't be underwater because I can't breathe underwater... *can I? But nothing else makes sense. Hold on. Breathing underwater doesn't make sense, either.*

I reached up with my hand and waved it in front of me. I could see little currents in the water as I moved it. There was my answer. I was underwater. I felt panic grip me again.

How am I breathing? How am I not dead? How am I not...

I did not get to finish my thoughts because the door in front of me opened and the man who had talked with me before, then had followed me into the coffee shop, and somehow got into my car — and kissed me, floated into the room in front of me.

Before I could even open my mouth to speak, the sight of him robbed me of thought... of speech... of sense. He was floating in front of me in gold and silver and some sort of... something I had no name for. His dark suit had been replaced by some sort of luminescent material that floated and clung in all the right places and was covered by strategically placed plates of what could only be armor. His short, dark hair floated out from his head just slightly underneath the brilliant crown that covered his head.

I could feel myself staring, my thoughts going fuzzy again as I looked at him. Resolutely, I closed my eyes and moved my head so I wouldn't see him if I opened my eyes again.

My thoughts mostly cleared, but not entirely. Obviously, this was not drugs. There was no drug on Earth I knew of that could make someone able to breathe underwater.

And, even more frightening, logic went right out the window with the reminder that I was somehow breathing underwater.

Apparently, I had lost my mind. That must be the answer. Or maybe it was drugs—and I was imagining all of this... this... very vivid fantasy.

"Do you have everything you need, my dear?" The muscles in my stomach tightened in response to his voice and my thoughts started to go fuzzy again. I seemed to be reacting to him unconsciously... or maybe subconsciously. Whatever it was, it annoyed me. He spoke and the heat of his voice sent a phantom caress all along my body.

I shook my head, trying to shake off whatever effect he was having on me. The thoughts that had, only moments ago, been solid and strong in my mind —were now just fog and smoke. I shook my head again, desperate to shake off his control and figure out what was going on. Something was not right here and I knew it. Somehow I had to figure it out and he was not going to stop me.

His hand came around my elbow and I could feel the heat coming from him again as if he were all around me. "What is it, my Queen? Are you unwell?"

Did he just call me his Queen?

Something about that felt very wrong, not at all how it was supposed to be.

What is going on?

I pushed away from him, and found myself floating easily. The heat of him cooled, but only a bit. I could tell that I would have to fight hard against it or he would have me under his spell again. I did my best to clear my throat, no easy thing since there was water filling my mouth, throat and lungs. It came out sounding like a strange gargling. Not precisely the serious, intimidating sound I had been looking for.

"What do you want with me?" My words came out easily enough, but they sounded different than I expected them to. I couldn't really remember how exactly they were supposed to sound. I just knew somehow that they were different.

He didn't answer. He simply floated there, in front of me, with an odd expression on his face. I could tell right away that at least part of it was annoyance. He was obviously not a man who was accustomed to being questioned—or ignored.

A moment later, I felt the heat again. It was

reaching out to me, wrapping itself around me, pulling me to him. It was binding me to him, making all of the thoughts in my head go fuzzy again. And inside... inside of me, there was heat as well.

I felt desire snaking through my body, awakening long dormant parts of my womanhood, wants and needs I had clearly suppressed for far too long. The most feminine parts of me were aroused by his nearness, his masculinity, his strength, by some indefinable quality that had anticipation filling my very core and a desire fighting to overwhelm me.

I struggled to remember why it was important to fight this feeling. A part of me wanted desperately to move toward him, wrap myself around him and surrender all of me.

But there was another part of me that still resisted. Though I didn't fully remember why, I held onto that tiny thread of resistance, pushing away the desire, shaking my head in an attempt to clear out the lustful thoughts that were trying to fill my thoughts.

And then he moved toward me again. The desire moving through me was like a silk rope that pulled me to him, even as he moved toward me. I was bound so tightly, I could do little more than hang on to the tiny thread in my mind that told me this was a very bad idea.

I wasn't sure why or how it could ever be a bad idea to give in to the temptation that was building within me, swallowing every other thought, flowing throughout my over-heated body.

On a gasp, my head dropped back a little as his arms came around me, his mouth a whisper from mine. There was something like triumph in his eyes and a shockingly pleased smile on his mouth that any other time—with any other man—would have made me want to slap him, but somehow made him even more desirable to me in this moment.

I struggled to maintain a rapidly weakening grip on my mind, a tiny thread of thought that caused me to wonder if he was doing something to make me feel this way—something that was overpowering even my most basic common sense.

But then his lips touched mine and the heat was blazing through me, burning from the inside out and fanning the flames of desire that were fighting to wipe away every coherent thought in my head.

A moment later, he angled his head a little to gain better access to my mouth, his lips moving over mine in some ancient ritual that was clearly meant to brand me as his. His arms wrapped tightly around my back, pulling me closer to his body, so much that I was pressed up against his armor, with no room for air or water between us. Meanwhile, my hands—without permission or prompting—reached up and took hold of his shoulders, curling around the strange fabric there, pulling him even closer to me.

Before I could stop or think, the impulses that seemed to be operating without my approval or control had me wrapped around him and we were floating... backwards.

His hands moved over my body as we floated and his mouth continued its assault on mine. He pulled me even closer than I had managed to do on my own as my legs tangled with his in the water that was beginning to feel like a sauna.

Everywhere his hands, lips and body touched mine, there was unimaginable heat. It rushed to my skin and melted all the way through to my bones. My skin felt like flames licked along every inch, whether he was touching me there or not. I was on a slow meltdown and I was beginning to think it just might be a good thing.

Somehow, the slight thud that was my backside colliding with the wall behind us managed to bring me to my senses enough that I twisted away and then managed to maneuver around him as he turned. I floated back and away from him, holding up both hands to ward him away.

"Stop." When he moved forward, I added, "Please." And for some reason, that stopped him.

"I don't know what you're doing, why you're doing this, what you want from me, but I don't belong here. I can't seem to remember much, but I do know that." I floated backwards until I hit the wall behind me with a little muffled thump, but he stayed where he was. His face was suddenly a mask of something akin to shame.

"I had hoped you would want to be here, to stay with me, to be my Queen." His words sounded very different, and every last bit of heat that had still been reaching out toward me suddenly melted away.

My thoughts became my own again and I was swamped with memories. Thoughts of my family, the day I had met him, what had happened before I blacked out—it all came back to me. Muscles in my chest tightened as I thought of my sweet babies, of losing them, of leaving them, of never seeing them again. If I stayed there with him, what would happen to them? What would they think had happened to me? How would they know I was safe, or cared for, or even alive?

I felt around where my pockets in my jeans were, desperate... thinking that perhaps if I could find my phone, I could send them a message. But there was nothing in my pockets—no phone, no keys, nothing.

Full on panic gripped me then. What would happen to my babies? There would be no explanation for where I had gone. Would they look for me?

Would they panic, mourn, let go and move on, or would they wonder if I had been taken against my will —and eventually sold to those who buy and sell human lives? Would they grow up thinking that I was somewhere... out there... unable to get back to them? How could they possibly handle it?

I began to feel angry with him. Who was he? Even better, just who did he think he was—kidnapping me!

How dare he do something like this to me?

Just what had he done to me? I wasn't supposed to be able to breathe underwater. Could I even go home again? Would I be able to live on land and breathe air again? What did he do to cause me to breathe underwater like this? Without my knowledge or permission, he had turned me into what? A fish?

How dare he!

The muscles in my chest constricted again, robbing me of this strange water breathing. Intense pain replaced the heat that had raced through me only moments ago. An icy cold flooded through my body as fear took hold of me.

I shook my head as I floated slowly to the floor, fighting the panic, desperately trying to breathe, black spots dancing in front of my eyes as he floated in front of me again.

"My babies..." My words trailed off as darkness closed in again, as the tightness in my chest won.

I heard him say something to me. A moment later, I thought I could feel his hands tugging at me, lifting me up, but before I could be sure of anything, the blackness pulled me back under again.

chapter three

I WAS FLOATING IN FRONT OF A FULL
-length mirror, watching as attendants moved around
me, pulling and moving pieces of an elaborate gown
and headdress they had assured me I would only have
to wear for a short time.

I was grateful to know this. Even with the near
weightlessness of floating, the layers of gold and
jewels pressed down on me. It weighed heavily on my
head, my arms, my body. And the gown was almost
ridiculously tight against my body, constricting my
movement and my breath.

I turned my head back and forth as I tried to get a
good look at the intricately carved crown that had

been fastened into my hair. Strands of it twisted over and around the base of it and thick, beautiful braids pulled through and around other parts of it.

I wondered what they had done to my hair to make it look so thick. Were all those braids really made from my hair or had something been woven into it to make the braids look fuller and longer?

Do I really have that much hair?

I tugged experimentally on one of the braids that hung down a little over my face. It certainly felt real enough. My tugging pulled at my scalp in several places and I quickly let go, not wanting any of the braid work to be damaged and need to be redone.

It was taking so long to complete. It was easily the most detailed part of the crown and surrounding headdress. If they started over, I knew I might be tempted to scream.

To distract myself, I turned my attention back to what the attendants were doing. One of them was busy attaching jewels in some sort of pattern to my tail. As I watched, the pattern emerged, though it didn't look like anything specific to me.

Perhaps it's like the tattoos.

Just the thought of the tattoos they had applied hours ago in patterns all over my skin made me shiver as I remembered the urge to squirm.

With my first involuntary movement, they had locked me into some sort of device that held me perfectly still, no matter how much I tried to move, and continued with the application. Every stroke of whatever they had been using to decorate my skin had tickled and had my muscles practically vibrating.

It was torture. I couldn't move away and I couldn't get them to stop. I'd had to actually bite my tongue at one point to stop myself from screaming. It had gone on for what felt like hours, and when they had finally released me, I had nearly fainted with relief, grateful that I floated easily, since by then my muscles felt as weak as the water moving around me.

Now they were imitating those patterns with jewels, and I twitched a little as one of the attendants' fingers brushed a ticklish area on my tail. I gritted my teeth, knowing that it would be better to endure it than to be locked into that strange contraption again.

No one had bothered to explain to me why all of these things were necessary. I had figured out on my own that they must have something to do with the ceremony. What little I had seen of the patterns that had been tattooed onto my skin looked like some sort of ancient symbols. Perhaps they had to do with the ceremony itself, binding me to the King in some special way.

No one had said anything and I was hesitant to ask, not wanting to look silly. Somehow I felt that I should know these things, but something had made my thoughts feel a bit fuzzy... *nerves perhaps*... and I didn't want anyone to think that I was not fit for this honor, after all. So I said nothing. I asked nothing. I held tight to the desire to resist those parts of the ceremony that felt odd or wrong.

This was a great honor, and I would do my best to be worthy of it. I was determined. I would not let the King down. I would be worthy of the crown that would sit upon my head.

I smiled down at the young attendant who bowed to me as she had apparently finished adjusting the jewels. Something about her was familiar. Had I seen her before today? I couldn't seem to remember. I nodded absently, returning her bow as I tried to figure out what about her was so familiar. *Why can't I remember?*

It was frustrating, but again I reminded myself that I did not want to do anything to appear unworthy of the great honor that was being bestowed upon me, so I tried to direct my mind elsewhere.

I looked again into the tall mirror, watching as the shimmering areas of my tail reflected and colors danced across the jewels that had been placed there.

Then, as I watched, the image changed. A young girl looked back at me, a smile on her face as she turned this way and that, admiring the tail that flowed down her body and then out behind her, a long piece of the same material flopping out from behind her feet from side to side as she turned. She giggled when she looked up and realized I was standing behind her.

"What do you think, Mommy?"

Before the words faded from my thoughts, I was

moving backward, struggling to keep calm and not hit any of the attendants who were still moving around me.

What was that? Who was that? What is going on?

There were no answers, but a sudden, unexpected panic was clawing at me now. Clearly, something had happened to my memory. It was not just fuzzy because of nerves.

I had no idea who that little girl was, but I felt such a strong attachment to her, I knew she must be important to me. So, where was she? Why was she not here? Why couldn't I remember her?

I wanted to ask someone, but something stopped me. There was such a strong sense that I must be calm, serene, regal, worthy of the great honor I was about to be given.

I shook my head. Why couldn't I remember the little girl? I searched my thoughts, trying to recall her, but someone's words kept repeating in my head whenever I questioned what was going on around me.

And this ceremony. Where had all of that come from? I knew it was of great importance. A great honor to be bestowed upon me, but why? It made no sense to me.

When I looked up, and opened my mouth to ask one of the attendants what was going on, I saw that the room around me was suddenly empty. Something about that could not be right. When did they leave? More importantly, why did they leave?

I moved toward the doorway, determined to find someone who could tell me what was happening.

There was no one in the corridor either, and though it felt strange to me that no one was around now, when there had been dozens of people filling the rooms only moments ago, I was determined to find some answers, so I moved out of the room and into the wide corridor.

I was careful to move slowly, not wanting to tip my headdress or mess up the lines of my skin-tight gown. Following the long corridor was proving to do nothing but frustrate me. At every corner I looked for someone—anyone—but there was no one there.

And then the man—who I somehow knew was the King—was there, suddenly in front of me, blocking my path. His eyes were filled with an emotion I was almost afraid to interpret. His expression was fierce, his natural charm radiating in almost visible waves from him.

A great heat washed over me like a storm with huge waves breaking over rocks. I stopped moving forward immediately, but I did not look down or away. If I was going to be his Queen, I needed to stand my ground. This could be a test. It would be one I would pass.

Staring him down was difficult. His expression seemed as though it was designed to bore into me, but I was determined to show him I was worthy.

After what felt like a very long time, but in reality

was only a few minutes, the muscles in his jaw relaxed a little, the expression in his eyes softened, and he floated a little less stiffly. "You sent away your attendants. Why... when you are not ready for the ceremony?"

I shook my head as I answered. "I didn't send anyone away." I backed up a little, as he moved forward quickly... unexpectedly, advancing on me with an even more fierce expression.

"You are using your abilities. You must learn to control them." His voice was harsh, causing me to cower and shrink back.

Then, as his words sunk in, I shook my head again and moved forward. "I don't know what you are talking about. What abilities? What control? What could I possibly do to send everyone away without knowing I've done it?"

"There are a number of abilities that come with your new station as Queen. Many of them you already possess, as an effect of your transformation. You must learn control. You've no idea of the power you wield, power over the seas themselves." His voice wasn't as fierce now, as he moved slowly toward me. He was close enough that I could feel little waves of water that his words pushed out toward me.

I started to speak, but stopped myself. I tried to think about what he had just said. What had he—or someone—done to transform me? Especially if I had abilities I didn't even know about. How was that even possible?

Why would he have transformed me? Were there special things I needed in order to be his Queen? Special abilities? Such as breathing underwater?

What has he done to me?

When I said nothing, he took hold of my arm and pulled me close. His grip was strong but not painful. Firm but not harsh. It left me feeling as if there was something I was missing... or something I was forgetting... again.

"What did you do to me? Why can't I remember? What is it you've made me forget? How did you do it? And why?" I leaned into him as I spoke, close enough to see nerves jump in his expression, to see his composure slip.

Good! Maybe I can get some answers now.

I could see it on his face. He looked as if he were fighting against a desire to speak. He knew the answers to all of my questions... perhaps even ones I had not thought to ask yet, but he was holding back.

Was it possible that I now possessed something like the ability he had used to charm me? Was it possible that I was using it instinctively somehow? Was he fighting against it? Could I force him to tell me?

It was then that I realized his charm was not affecting me now as it had before. I could still feel waves of it emanating from him, but I felt no desire whatsoever to obey, to acquiesce, to bend to his will. I felt powerful, strong, irresistible.

I like this feeling!

I attempted to tap into whatever part of me was controlling the waves of heat that were flowing freely from me now. It was several seconds before I felt confident that I had found the way to control it. When I did, I did everything I could to turn up the power.

I want — I need — answers.

"Stop. I did not give you these abilities so that you could use them against me." He floated backwards, his eyes filled with something like betrayal now.

"Then answer my questions!" I waited, turning down the power a little and at the same time, trying to explore the part of my mind that felt as if I had never had access to it before.

Suddenly I knew how I had made the servants disappear. I knew that I was still sending a wave out from my mind, telling them to stay away. I wondered why... why my mind had decided to send the servants away, but that information was not in the same place as the how.

At that moment, the image of the young girl in the mirror came back to me. I gasped and floated backward. There was something about that child. I knew she was special, but I still couldn't seem to figure out how or why — or who she was.

I concentrated all of my attention, all of my focus, all of my determination on the memory of that little girl, desperate now to figure out who she was, where she was, and why I remembered her, but couldn't make out who she was.

I ignored the man in front of me. I ignored the strange message I was evidently still broadcasting to all of the servants without knowing how or why. I ignored all the other questions that roared inside my mind for answers. I held on to the image of her face, started to think of names, trying to place them with her and sort out if I knew her name as well.

Cassie!

Her name was like an explosion in my mind. And then, thoughts and memories were washing over me like waves, filling my mind with so much, I wanted to scream.

A thousand images flipped through my head at a dizzying speed, each one accompanied by emotions and knowledge. It was impossible to hold onto any one thing. The onslaught sent me to my knees on the smooth floor of the corridor. I felt as if I was being pressed into the floor by the sheer weight of everything coming at me like a massive storm assaulting the shoreline.

And then I did scream. The pain in my mind, in my heart, in my entire being—from the memories, from the assault, the agony of my separation from them all —it was too much for me. I screamed, and pain ripped through me. The sound deafened me. The effort drained me.

And then I stopped screaming. Something within

me had shifted and it felt as if the breath had been knocked out of me. It was as if I was being suffocated. The water was swirling around me in a strange mass of cold and darkness. It pressed into me, crushing me with an unrelenting weight. It swallowed up any hope of sound. There was nothing but the mass of water and darkness. I gasped for air, for anything, but nothing helped. I reached out, desperate to find something I could hold onto, something that would stop the spinning, but there was only water.

And then, suddenly I was standing... on my feet and legs... with no tail... on dry land, in front of a house—my house. All of my memories—every single one—came crashing back in on me like a tidal wave. I dropped to my knees on the hard concrete.

I could finally remember the day I had been missing... maybe not all of it, but most of it. There were still a lot of pieces that were blurry, probably the parts where the King—or one of his minions—had been doing whatever it was that was done to me to make me feel insanely attracted to him.

I could remember being in a store, bumping into him, feeling light-headed and giggly over him. I could remember making as quick an escape as I could and then I had gone to get coffee.

He had been there, too. He had held the door for me, then followed me in, all the time using his abilities —his charm—to make me feel giddy over him, to throw me off balance, to strengthen my attraction.

Then he had gotten into my car, kissed me, and somehow he had transported us to a shipwreck.

In the shipwreck, he'd done something to me, somehow made me able to breathe underwater. He'd changed me into something else. With that thought, I started to panic again. I was back on dry land. Would I be able to breathe?

I took an experimental breath. The air moved into my mouth and then down my throat. It obviously did whatever it normally did from there. I exhaled, and breathed in again. Everything felt like it was supposed to. After a few more breaths, I pushed that concern to the back of my mind. I would figure out later what it all meant. Clearly, whatever he had done in the shipwreck had changed me, but since I could breathe on land, it could wait.

When I thought about what he had done to me, I thought about the heat that had come from him. I knew it was an ability of his... charm, he called it. I knew he had power over me, but in my mind now it all felt different than it had at the time.

Somehow if felt as if his charm no longer had the same effect on me as it had when I first met him. Either I had built up some sort of tolerance to it or the changes he had made gave me an immunity of sorts. Either way, it gave me hope. If he showed up again — and I was certain he would — I would not be so easily overwhelmed again.

With a feeling that I might not have a lot of time

before he showed up again, I turned my attention to the house in front of me. How long had I been gone? I had no way of knowing. Had it been hours or days... or even weeks? I could have been unconscious for some time each time I had blacked out.

Who knows how long it took to do whatever it was that was done to me?

chapter four

I STOOD IN FRONT OF THE HOUSE, hesitating on the sidewalk in front, looking at the green shutters, the grey door, the freshly mowed lawn and the little flag whipping in the light breeze.

This was home... my home... my family's home.

I was sure of it.

But without knowing how long I had been gone, I was more than a little hesitant to just walk in. I had no explanations to offer my family, no idea of how I had gotten here—or what had been done to me—and no idea of how much time I had until I would have to face him again. And no idea what he might do to me or my family if—or when—he showed up.

Once again, panic started to press in on me, but it was different than I was coming to expect. Something within me kept it from overwhelming me this time, almost like I had put it in a little box that I could open whenever I felt like it. It helped tremendously.

"Mom?"

This voice was familiar, and when I looked at the face that went with it, I nearly screamed again, though in delight this time. I started to move forward, but her expression stopped me. She just stood there, staring at me. She didn't look frightened—more perplexed than anything—and I found myself worrying that I might look odd or different somehow. But, since I had no way of seeing myself, I just stood there watching as several emotions played across her face.

She was definitely concerned, but not panicked. For the first time I had hope that maybe I hadn't been gone that long—and maybe I didn't look all that different. Maybe she was reacting to the clothes I was wearing and the weird headdress.

Then, she looked behind me. "Where's your car, Mom?" Her words were laced with concern and filled with confusion.

Where was my car? I wasn't really sure. Was it still parked at the coffeehouse? Had he just left it there, or had he used it to transport me somewhere and left it there?

He certainly hadn't driven it underwater.

The memory of his kiss slammed into me, an explosion of heat and desire churned within me and I nearly gasped from the strength of it. Whatever he had done with that kiss was obviously different from the ability to charm me with the heat that flowed from him. It appeared that I had no immunity to that kiss. Even the memory of it was enough to make me weak in the knees—and somewhere deep inside me something was reaching out to him, calling to him— desperate for his touch.

I watched as my daughter moved forward, but there was no sound aside from the sudden roar in my ears. What was going on? Was my body doing more than reaching out to him? Was I trying to go to him— somehow?

I forced my thoughts away from him, from his kiss, from the thought of getting to him. I focused on my daughter.

"Mom, what was that? What just happened?" Her voice was full of something... not panic, but more than curiosity... something akin to awe and excitement.

I shook my head. I had no idea how to answer her —and as I was still trying to clear my head of the intense desire that had taken hold of me, I was a little afraid to speak.

When I realized I had dropped to my knees again, I stood. My legs were shaky, but held me up well enough. When I looked down at them, thinking that something wasn't right, I saw that I was still wearing the gown the palace attendants had put me in. That would mean I still had the headdress, too.

No wonder she was looking at me weird. I probably look like some underwater attraction from an aquarium show.

"Where have you been, Mom? And what's going on? Is everything all right?" For the first time, she sounded concerned and I couldn't exactly blame her. I had disappeared for who knew how long. And now, I'd shown up in a weird outfit and most likely soaking wet.

Absently, I ran a hand over the skirt of my gown.

That's strange...

It wasn't wet. The material was like nothing I'd ever felt, but it was dry... completely dry. Also, as I ran my hand over it, I realized I could feel the bumps underneath where the attendant had affixed jewels to my tail.

To my tail... I had a tail. How did I have a tail? Where did it go? What happened to me?

The panic was clawing at me again, and this time it was less easy to control.

"Mom!" Cassie's voice distracted me just enough that the panic receded. She was shouting. Why was she shouting.

"Whatever it was that happened a minute ago was happening again. Mom, it was water. I don't know how to explain it, but there was water swirling around you just now. It looked like it was going to swallow you up. What... How... Why..." She stopped for a second, took a deep breath, and started again. "Mom, what is happening?"

I dropped to my knees again, suddenly feeling completely drained of all energy. When she stepped forward, and reached out to steady me, I gasped "I wish I knew" and then everything turned black.

When I woke again, I was in my own bed. I knew before I moved, before I even looked around, exactly where I was. The bed was as familiar to me as my own reflection. The mattress fit around me just like it had for nearly ten years, though it was not quite so comfortable anymore as it had been. I snuggled down into the familiar impressions, doing my best to shut out everything that had happened over a length time I still had no actual measure of.

Lying there, comfortable and breathing easily, I started to wonder if there was a chance I had just dreamed it all. Was it possible that I had? It had certainly felt real, but here I was... in my own bed, as if it had never happened.

Could it be possible, that I had not yet gone to the store or the coffee shop? Perhaps I had gone to sleep thinking about it, dreading it, and my mind had cooked up this little adventure to make the whole thing feel less daunting.

Then I rolled onto my back, and a flash of light caught my attention. I blinked several times, trying to clear the sleep remnants that typically caused my vision to be blurry first thing after waking up. When I looked again, I could see there was something laying across the chair in my room, so I focused in on it.

The muscles in my chest clenched as if the breath had been knocked out of me.

There... on the chair in my room, in plain sight of anyone, was the gown and headdress my mother and daughter must have taken off of me before tucking me into bed. The piece that was catching a shaft of light that was coming in through the window happened to be the crown; more specifically, one of the jewels on the crown.

I threw the covers off and swung my legs over the edge of the bed, and gasped. My legs were a tail... a shimmery, scaly, full-on mermaid tail. As I watched, it flopped a little against the floor, then settled. I stared down at it for several seconds before I heard a noise outside my door. Then I was struggling to get it back up on the bed and under the covers before anyone came into the room.

I had just flipped the covers over it when the door opened, and in rushed everyone.

My daughter practically threw herself at me.

"Mom, we were so worried. We were almost ready to call an ambulance, but Grandma said you just needed some rest." She hugged me tightly and I prayed I would not lose my balance and tip over. If any part of that tail peeked out from under the covers, they would expect an explanation and I didn't have one.

I looked up at my mother and mouthed a quick "thank you" to which she just nodded.

When my son sat on the edge of the bed, I tried to moved the tail, but the intense pinch I felt where my knees should have been told me I hadn't succeeded. I tried to steel myself against the pain without showing it, but my expression must have given me away because he stood up very quickly only a second later.

"Oops. Sorry, Mom. Thought I missed your legs."

I took a deep breath, let it out and tried to answer calmly. "It's fine. You almost did."

I scooted as my daughter sat beside me on the bed, then panicked a little when I realized part of the tail was sticking out from under the covers.

"I hope you feel better, Mom. You slept all night and most of the morning." She played with my hair while I tried to gently ease the tail back under the covers. Unfortunately, it was not cooperating. The covers were stubbornly staying where they were, scooting along right on top of the tail.

"Oh, like you never sleep half the morning away." Dylan nudged his sister, laughing as he teased her. I tried pushing the tail back off the bed, hoping the covers would flop over and down with gravity.

"Oh shush, you." Cassie told her her brother, and I jumped a little at the closeness of her voice. A second later, she asked again, "You do feel better, don't you, Mom?"

I answered sort of absently as I tried to push the covers a little with my hand, trying to make it look like I was just smoothing them out. "Yes, sweetheart. I feel much better. Thank you."

"What is that!" Cassie launched herself off the bed, rushing around to the other side to pull the covers off the tail I was so desperately trying to hide. "Wow! This is great, Mom. Can I have one?"

I exhaled slowly, extremely grateful for the moment that she hadn't actually figured out it wasn't precisely what she thought it was. I sat there for a bit too long trying to decide what to tell her about whether or not she could have one of her own. I couldn't very well tell her she could have one. I didn't even know how I had one... much less how to get rid of it.

"Wow. If I didn't know any better, I would think this was a real tail." She was running her hands all over it, pausing a little over each jewel that was still firmly attached.

I laughed a little in reply, but said nothing, desperately afraid that she would discover the truth in her words any second now.

"Even I have to admit it's pretty cool, Mom.

Where'd you get it?" This came from Dylan, who stood by the bed looking down at the tail with an odd sort of respect.

I just sat there. I had no idea what to say. Once upon a time, I had looked for man-made Mermaid tails for Cassie online, but none of the store names came to mind as I searched frantically through my memories of flipping through page after page of pretty tails made from swimsuit or scuba suit materials.

"Hey! You found one without a hole where the fin goes. How did you..." She trailed off as she raised and lowered the fin at the very bottom of the tail, seeing for the very first time the veins that ran underneath the surface of the tail and the way it was positioned over where my feet should have been. "Mom?" She looked at me then with an odd expression, part fascination, part fear.

I could only nod.

She gasped and stepped back, dropping the fin on the tail I was beginning to worry might actually be a permanent change, essentially a side effect of whatever he had done to me... further evidence that it had not been a dream.

My mother walked over, picked up the fin part of my tail, looked at it very closely, and then set it gently back down on the bed.

"So, the outfit, the crown..." She motioned behind her and I nodded. "I think it's time you told us exactly what happened yesterday, sweetheart." There was something in her voice; not fear precisely, more like sadness.

I shook my head a little before speaking. "I don't really know what happened, Mom. I went to the store to get those prices for you." She nodded and I went on, wiping unexpected tears from my eyes. "While I was there, I bumped into this man, and it was weird." I shook my head a little, trying not to let my brain go back to the feeling too much. I certainly didn't want him showing up here, with my family all right there with me. And I had a strong suspicion he could do it.

"Anyway, when I bumped into him, it felt like something kind of scrambled my thoughts. He helped me over to sit down and asked me if I was all right. I told him I was, but I really didn't feel all right. I felt... weird."

My mother broke in there. "Was that when... whatever this is... happened to you?" She gestured toward the tail and then the crown and gown laying across my chair as she spoke.

I shook my head. "Not then. Actually, he left me sitting there. I took those pictures for you and then left. It was after that, when I went to the coffee shop..." I stopped and waved away whatever Mom had been preparing to say. "I know. I know." She was always saying the coffee shop was going to be my downfall. "But it wasn't like that. It's not really anything to do with the coffee shop. It just happened there."

"Uh huh."

She laughed, but said nothing else. I took a deep breath and jumped back into my explanation.

"After I picked up my drink, I went back out to the car. He followed me, and before I could figure out what he meant to do, he got in."

"Didn't you have the doors locked?" That stopped me, and I tried to think back to the moment just before he had opened the door and gotten in. Had I unlocked all of the doors or just mine?"

"Actually, I did."

I could remember worrying about his odd behavior. I had made a point to only click the remote one time. The passenger side door would have stayed locked. So how had he gotten in?

I had no answer.

"So, he got into a locked car somehow?"

I nodded, and when Mom said nothing else, I went on.

"Anyway, after that, I blacked out. I woke up somewhere weird."

"Wait. Wait." Mom held up a hand as she interrupted. "You blacked out? Why? How?"

I looked down as I answered. "Well..." I hesitated, but I could feel the heat of three expectant looks on the top of my head, so I went on, the words getting quieter as I went on. "... he kissed me and everything just went black."

I could feel heat creeping up to fill my cheeks. It

was beyond embarrassing to admit to my mother — and my children — that a man's kiss had made me lose consciousness, but it wasn't as if he were a regular man. As far as I knew, he was a King. But how his title or position could have had anything to do with what happened to me, I had no idea.

"All right." She looked around her, at the two teens who were watching me with more attention than they gave everything else I said to them. "I think I understand. Move ahead."

"Well, there's a lot of the same sort of stuff in what happened next. Just let me say that I woke up somewhere weird and he showed up and I blacked out again and then I woke up somewhere even weirder."

Mom was shaking her head at me, her expression inscrutable. "This somewhere weird... It wouldn't happen to be one of those aquariums where they do the mermaid shows, would it?"

I laughed. I couldn't help it. "No, it wasn't an aquarium. It's kind of hard to explain, and I'm trying really hard not to think too much about it, but the second time I woke up, my memories were all scrambled again — only more. It was like I didn't even remember who I really was."

"And you had a tail?" This came from Dylan, who was no longer looking at the tail like it was something cool.

"Yes, Dylan, then I had the tail." A second later, I

added, "The second time I woke up, not the first." I wasn't certain why I felt the need to clarify, but I did... so... I did.

"But you didn't have the tail when you came back home." This came from Cassie. She was still looking at the tail like it was special... and like she wanted one. If only I could figure out how to give it to her instead of having it myself...

"I know I didn't. I don't know how it went away or I would do it right now." I looked down at the shimmery, scaly thing that had completely taken the place of my legs. How had I done this? How could I undo it? Would I ever find out what he had done to me?

With that thought, something inside of me shifted and I knew... somehow... that he was on his way.

"Um, guys..." I did not get a chance to finish what I was going to say, because a thick column of water appeared in the room in front of us. It appeared to flow from ceiling to floor and the water contained within was rushing so quickly, there was no way to see past it.

But I knew... somehow... that it was him. I watched my hand as it reached out on its own, stretching toward the water without my permission.

chapter five

BEFORE I COULD TOUCH THE WATER, however, it disappeared. Left behind where it had just been, he stood. The man. The "King", complete with legs and dressed in the same fancy suit I had seen him wearing the first time I bumped into him at the store. He also looked to be completely dry.

His hand was stretched out toward mine, and though it was no easy thing, since it did not want to obey, I was able to pull my hand back to my side— quickly—before he could take hold of me. His response was a gruff sigh as his hand dropped to his side.

He stood there, looking at me, for several seconds

that felt as if each second was stretched out to an hour or more. As time passed, it felt almost as if everything around me was being muffled, as if his intense gaze was somehow blinding me to everything and everyone around me.

I tried to look away, to close my eyes, to shake my head, but nothing worked. It was as if I had lost all control of my body. I was mesmerized by his eyes, and rapidly losing sight of everyone in the world who was important to me.

My heart began to pound in my chest, just as breathing became difficult. It was all too familiar. I struggled internally, panic starting to take hold of me. The thought of losing my memories of my family again was too frightening to deal with.

"Are you ready to come home now?" His voice was that of someone speaking to a child. I didn't care for it.

"I am home." I answered simply.

I would never win if I tried to best him. I knew that. He was far too powerful for me. I might not understand the hold he seemed to have over me, but I did not doubt it's strength. And I might have been able to use whatever abilities I had now against him before, but something told me he would not let me get the better of him again. The only option I might have was to stand my ground and hope it was enough.

He stood there looking at me for perhaps twenty seconds before Cassie stepped between us. "You can't take her anywhere." Her voice was full of venom and attitude, more than I had ever heard from her before.

I started to move forward, only remembering the tail that would stop me from standing when I was nearly there. Surprisingly, nothing stopped me from standing. I got to my feet with no trouble at all, placing a hand of support on my daughter's shoulder, not daring to look down for fear that the blasted tail might make a reappearance, but looking straight ahead, lifting my shoulders and inclining my head instead of just looking up at him... no easy task since he was easily a foot taller than I stood—tail or no tail.

The expression on his face gave me the impression that I was little more than an annoyance at the moment. Determined to stand my ground, and also somewhat driven to show him that I could be a great deal more frustrating if I needed to be, I simply stood there behind Cassie, staring him down.

I was working to put all of the emotions, all of the anger I'd felt over the last few minutes, all of the frustration when I'd started to remember my family, when I'd somehow found a way to leave and come home, into my own expression.

After several very long, very tense seconds of the four of us standing there; clearly at a stalemate, my mother turned to me. When she turned, she was already opening her mouth to speak. However, what came out was not speech, but a shriek. And then she was turning toward the bed beside me, nearly knocking me down in the process.

From Cassie I heard a gasp. From my son, a groan. And then my mother was wrapping the light blanket from my bed around me as my son made a quick and discreet exit from the room.

"What..." was all I managed to get out before I realized I was completely naked underneath the blanket.

Color leaped into my cheeks. I had been standing there, in front of a man I barely knew—and my teenage son—without a single item of clothing on. And I had been staring at him all this time, trying to look intimidating.

Intimidating... hah! Only if flab and stretch marks are intimidating.

As the heat in my cheeks continued to flame, I looked down at the floor, trying to figure out if there was some way I could sink into it, or maybe just force myself to faint so I wouldn't have to deal with the fallout that was certainly coming.

Well, at least he's not one of those men who has no self control.

From somewhere in my head, the thought emerged, and while I didn't really want to give him credit for being somewhat decent, I had to admit it was impressive that he had stood there staring at my face, and not my naked, flabby body.

Then I was trying to distract myself and figure out exactly how I had ended up standing there with absolutely no clothes on. Had I gone to bed naked? Had no one thought to put pajamas on me when they had taken the gown off of me last night before putting me to bed? Had my clothes somehow disappeared with the tail... or had the tail showing up somehow made my clothes disappear?

Or did he do it somehow?

I'd rather blame him, and besides, that thought made the most sense. He had been doing weird things to me all along; with my memory, with my body, with my thoughts and my reactions. I was also fairly certain he was somehow responsible for the tail. I just didn't know how to prove it.

"Mom, where did your cool tail go? When did you take it off?" Cassie was completely unconcerned with my lack of clothing, clearly more preoccupied with the missing tail.

She moved around me and started pulling at the covers left on the bed. My mother, thankfully, started pushing at the man in front of me, shooing him out of the room with her typical parental authority.

The last thing I saw before she closed the door in front of his face was an expression so comical, it left me laughing... almost hysterically.

If only I could figure out how to do what my mother had done... but I knew there was little hope. Dylan was fifteen and I had yet to learn to imitate my mother in any of the parental ways that got the sort of results she just had.

Even though I was naked—and I knew I would have to deal with the man currently being intimidated by my mother, I sank down onto the bed for a moment, if for no other reason than to catch my breath.

Evidently I had only been gone a day... or actually less than a day, if Mom was asking me what had happened the day before—and apparently I had slept all night and most of the current morning...

Regardless of time, my head was reeling with everything that had happened. Just what had occurred already today would have been enough to have me spinning out, but when I put it with everything else—it was a wonder I wasn't curled up in a tiny little ball of weeping mess.

I barely looked up, barely registered the sound of the door opening, until Cassie was pulling at the blanket that was still loosely wrapped around me.

"Mom, what happened to the tail? How did you make it go away? Why did you make it go away? It was really cool. Was it really real? Like, could you swim underwater with it and everything? It looked like it was stuck on really good—I mean with glue or something. How did you do that? And if it was glued on, how did you get it off so fast?"

I looked up at her, and there must have been something in my expression; panic, fear, something... because she stopped talking and launched herself at me, wrapping her arms so tightly around me that it was almost painful.

I didn't complain. In fact, I pried my own arms out of the blanket and returned her embrace, holding her as close as I could — and burying my nose in her sweet smelling hair.

With the smell of coconut and what I always thought of as beach filling up my sense of smell, more memories of my precious daughter flooded back into my mind. Things I hadn't even missed before when the initial onslaught had swamped me. There were so many images of my sweet little girl and her beloved ocean.

We had only been to the beach a handful of times in her short life, but she always spent as much time as possible on the beach or in the water. Any other time in her life, it nearly took a crowbar to pry her from her bed in the mornings. But not at the beach. Whenever we were at the beach, she would somehow hear me when I woke to go out and enjoy the sunrise. She would slip out of bed, changing her clothes quickly and quietly while I slipped into the bathroom — and be waiting for me when I stepped out, following happily along, wearing my extra sunglasses so the brightness of the early morning sun didn't burn her eyes.

We would stand there, hand in hand, watching the magnificent beauty of a new day as it crept up and over the water, filling the sky with the most incredible colors the human eye could see.

Sometimes we took a camera, trying to capture the brilliance—though a man-made lens could only do so much to record such beauty. But most mornings, we simply stood there, watching and enjoying the moment together.

When the colors had faded into the soft blues and grays of early morning and the sun was fully up in the sky, we would watch the beach a few minutes—laughing at the antics of the birds swooping in for an early morning meal and marveling at the resolve of joggers who had been out and about even before we'd gotten up.

We would laugh about silly things all the way back to the room and then make breakfast. Usually, we would sit out on the balcony to eat—and listen to the waves and the gulls as they swooped and called to each other in the early morning stillness.

Then, once everyone else was awake, Cassie would drag us down to the beach to swim and play in the sand. She'd always been the first one ready to go, the first to run into the cold water, and the last to be pulled away. Only the threat of not coming back down that day could actually get her to leave.

So, it was no surprise that she—who had always wanted to be a mermaid—was only interested in where the tail had gone and why I didn't seem to be as excited about it as she would have been if she were the one in my situation.

When I felt her shifting restlessly a little, I let go

and sat back. She didn't say anything else, but she did wrap her fingers in the blanket, twirling a little piece of it around her fingers and looking down at it as she tightened and loosened her grip. Clearly she wanted to ask more, but had figured out that it would just freak me out again.

I decided to go with truth, but keep it as simple as I could.

"I don't know where the tail went, sweetie. I don't know how or why it appeared and I know it's exciting for you, but I gotta be honest with you. It's a little scary for me because I don't know. I don't know this man or why he took me away—and I'm really worried he's going to try and take me away again."

She grabbed my hand then, wrapping her fingers tightly around my hand. "He can't take you away. He can't. I won't let him."

I squeezed back, trying to reassure her as much as myself. I couldn't make myself say the words that I somehow knew would be a lie, because I knew there was absolutely no way to guarantee or promise anything in this situation. He had already proved that he could take me without my permission and that he would go to some pretty extreme lengths to make me stay with him.

However, something had to be done. I knew that as well. I couldn't just hide in here and hope it all went away. I had to face him... deal with him... hopefully, convince him that my place was here with my family.

Reluctantly, I dropped the blanket, stood and went in search of clothes.

chapter six

WHEN I WALKED INTO THE LIVING room a few minutes later, my mother looked both appalled and approving of the clothing I had chosen. Clearly, her ingrained Southern hospitality did not approve of the ragged tee I had paired with pants that were so well-worn, the color had completely faded in several spots—and there were multiple spots that had obviously been repaired. I usually only wore these clothes when it was just the family around—and we weren't planning to leave the house—and we were doing some deep cleaning with things like bleach and I didn't want to ruin any other clothes.

Which was precisely why I had chosen them. I had also pulled my hair back in a messy ponytail and had on zero makeup. There was absolutely no way he could find me even the slightest bit attractive this way. No one could have.

Though, from the look he gave me when I dared face him, I might have overestimated myself. He had stood at my entrance. I realized that immediately. I also realized that, once again, he was not looking at my body.

Which meant my really had outfit did not have the impact I'd been hoping for anyway.

He was looking directly at my face. At my eyes. He was not yet using whatever supernatural ability he had used before, for which I was thankful, but he was staring pretty intensely—and I had absolutely no idea what to make of it.

I wanted to shout, *What is it about me? I mean me?*

But I somehow felt pretty certain that I would not like the answer—if, in fact, he even gave me one. He might well just repeat something I'd already heard—or come out with something equally dumb, like what a great honor he was bestowing upon me and how grateful I should be.

Which I am not.

With that in mind, I opened my mouth to speak, but he beat me to it.

"We should speak alone."

I was already shaking my head—and my mother

had stood, quickly aligning herself with me. I could hear Cassie moving to stand beside me, too. A moment later, her hand slipped into mine again, her fingers squeezing as if she could somehow keep me here just with the tightness of that grip.

I squeezed back, determined to reassure my baby girl, even though I knew that if he wanted to take me, the most powerful grip she could muster would not hold me here against his power.

"Whatever you have to say to me can be said in front of my family." I said the words with confidence, but the way that his expression changed made me regret my words.

He looked at me as if we were alone, in a bedroom, naked, and both desperate to... to consummate this ridiculous relationship. Before Cassie could have a chance to wonder... or ask what that look meant, I let go of her hand and gently pushed her behind me.

"Stop that. You know that is not what I meant."

He didn't stop though. And he didn't turn on his supernatural charm... heat... thing, but I felt almost as if he had. The temperature in the room felt as if it were moving up to steamy. Little tendrils of desire snaked their way through me. The desire in his eyes, the slightly crooked smile that was not even a little friendly, the suggestive tilting of one eyebrow, the slight shift in his body towards me—every piece of his expression and his body language told me precisely what he was thinking, what he was imagining right this moment. And, if he opened his mouth and actually said anything about it, my sweet little girl would be horrified.

So, I did what any mother would do. I caved. "All right, fine. Outside."

He smiled then, wolfishly triumphant.

I pushed a finger into his chest, hard. "But get this. I am not going anywhere with you—and if you try to take me, we both know I can fight your powers. We'll be right back here, doing this again and again and again until you get it through your thick skull that I will not be manipulated."

Those words obviously both shocked and confused him. He offered no resistance, no promises, but no insistence that he would have his way as he reached for my hand.

I stepped back instinctively. "What are you doing?

Again, he looked very confused. "Taking you outside."

I couldn't help myself. I nearly laughed at the seriousness of his expression. Had he seriously never used a door before?

I struggled with the smile that would have given me away as I answered him, infusing my voice with more than a little southern twang. I didn't laugh. I wasn't smiling, but I was still going to have some fun at his expense. "Around these parts we generally use the door to go outside." When he looked at me, confused again, I pointed, waving my arm just a little theatrically as I did.

With a long-suffering sigh, he turned and headed for the door. He didn't struggle with the doorknob when he reached it, just turned it, opened the door and walked through—which told me he had used a door before. More questions... At this rate, I might have too many questions to ever have even half of them answered.

With a sigh of my own, I followed him out the door. My mother made a noise as I moved away, but I kept going.

Once we were outside, I walked around to the side of the house that would afford us the most privacy. Fortunately, he followed with no argument.

However, the moment I stopped and turned to face him, he pulled me up onto my toes and into his arms, his lips capturing mine on a protest. He took advantage of my open mouth in the most delightful way, taking the kiss deeper until my head was filled with fog and my body was on fire. In that moment, everything else slipped from my mind, floated away into the fog. I forgot everything... everything but the desire to get closer to him, to have him go on doing what he was doing to me... forever.

Every part of me yearned to be closer to him, a desire he seemed to share—as he pulled me even closer, backing me up against the wall of the house so he could free his hands to move across my body. Everywhere he touched, heat followed... through the

71

layers of clothes I had pulled on in a desperate attempt to protect myself from him, igniting my already burning skin until I felt like one never-ending flame of desire and desperation.

Our lips never parted. We never separated for air, but only a tiny part of my brain even noticed, so intent was I on what he was doing to the rest of my body. I arched into his hands, reaching up with my hands to take hold of his shoulders, partially to keep my balance, partially to keep myself upright. The fog in my brain had spread to my legs... my knees especially. I was more than a little concerned that I just might slide to the ground.

He continued to ravish me in a most delightful way, with a single-mindedness that would likely surprise me later, when I could think straight again. For the moment, all I could seem to concentrate on was the amount of heat running along my skin and underneath it.

Every time I started to think I couldn't stand anymore, somehow... I did, but the heat continued to build. The flames danced. My knees buckled. My legs turned to jelly. And somehow, I stayed right where I was, still pushing to get closer.

How long we went on like that, I had no idea. The longer we kissed, the longer his hands roamed, the hotter the flames burned, the less I noticed time or the need for air or anything around us at all.

All of my senses were filled with him, smell, taste,

touch, hearing, even sight... every time I opened my eyes just a little, he was right there filling my vision. And it was only ever a few seconds before my eyes drifted shut again.

Sometime later, he slowed his hands, retreating little by little until he was barely kissing me, letting go and then letting his lips brush against mine again several times. He didn't step away, but he did pull me away from the wall behind me, back into his arms.

When he didn't kiss me for several seconds, I finally managed to open my eyes and look up him.

His eyes were still full of desire, heavy and dark, and looking down at my lips... as if he could do it all over again, any second.

"Are you ready to go home, now?"

It was like a tidal wave of ice cold water slamming into me. I had let him do precisely what I had promised myself I would not. I had let that charm of his, the power that must be supernatural, overwhelm me, nearly pull me away from my family—again.

I sidestepped, wobbling on legs that were still more than a little weak, but held me up enough.

"I told you. I am home." I swept a hand toward the house behind me. "This is my home. This is where my family is, where my life is. I can't leave them. I won't leave them."

When he started to step close again, I put a hand up, pushed against his chest, struggled to ignore the heat that was nearly burning my hand, wrapping around my wrist, working its way into my veins.

I lost my patience then. "Stop it." I knew there was a chance he might not be doing it on purpose... that it could very well be something that just happened, but I'd had enough. "Just stop it." I'd had it with the situation, with not having control over my own body, with half my memories still feeling like a scrambled mess, with the stupid tail that I didn't seem to have control over at all. And I'd had it with his crazy power over me.

"Seriously. Stop it." I repeated myself for the third time when I felt absolutely no change in the amount of heat still snaking its way up my arm.

And, for the first time since I had first met him, the heat stopped completely, shut off like he'd flipped a switch. And his face... it was a mask of frustration as he stepped back. "How is this possible? I do not understand."

His deep voice, which was usually strong and commanding, the voice of someone who was supposed to be King of the seas... was full of frustration on many levels. It also held more than a little anger, but mostly confusion. Had he always gotten his way?

I watched him. He looked completely and absolutely perplexed. He truly had no idea how I was resisting him. Or why... why I would ever do such a thing.

Honestly, I had no idea how I was resisting him. Not only did the ridiculous charm... heat... thing he did make me want to find a bedroom somewhere and not let go of him until both of us were utterly worn out.

His kisses were stunning, and everything about him screamed that he was so far out of my league it was crazy... I was crazy. To say no to him. To refuse him. To resist him.

What was so wrong with being attracted to him, anyway? I tried to think of something, but nothing came.

"Are you doing that, too?" I shook my head, trying to clear the lustful thoughts and fantasies that had started to weave themselves around how positively perfect he was in every way.

No. Stop that.

I told myself he was doing something... or that his powers of persuasion were somehow making my brain screwy again, but nothing seemed to work, so I side-stepped again and moved as far away as I could while staying close enough that we could talk without shouting.

"I mean it, stop it. Stop whatever you're doing. Right now."

And, oddly enough, it did stop... sort of. All of the thoughts about him that had been floating around in my brain since I'd first met him were there, but no new ones showed up and the crazed desire to crawl over to him and beg him to take me... right here, right now... finally began to subside.

I wasn't sure if that was a good thing or not. I really wanted my way with him—and for him to have his way with me. But I couldn't have things both ways. I couldn't tell him to stop touching me, while begging him to keep touching me.

For the first time since I had met him, I finally felt like I could begin to think straight again. "Thank you." I breathed the words, slowly, as my equilibrium finally began to return.

"I confess, I do not understand. Why do you ask me to stop? Do you not enjoy what I am doing?"

I shook my head, but no answer came to me, so I said nothing.

"You are not attached to anyone... is that correct? Am I mistaken? Is there a man you are attached to, bound to?"

I shook my head again, struggling not to laugh at his wording. "No. I'm not attached to anyone."

When he started to step forward, I pushed again. "But that does not mean I'm just yours to take. That's not how things work."

He completely ignored my words, the second set of words I'd spoken, choosing to concentrate on the first answer I'd given him.

"I do not understand. If you are not attached, why do you object to what I am doing? I can feel that you are attracted to me. You do not wish to become Queen of the Sea?"

"No, that's not it either." I answered slowly,

weighing each word as I spoke, trying to make him understand without offending him. I knew better than most just how delicate men's egos were.

"I have a life here. My children, my family, my work is here." When he started to speak, I held up a hand. When he stopped, I went on. "You took me away from them, tried to make me forget them." I held my hands up then, uncertain of what to say or do next, certain that if he hadn't gotten it by now, he never would.

"But you did not forget them."

I shook my head again. "I did, a little. Your hold over me was almost enough to make me forget them. I can't have that." I stopped for a moment. I could feel my temper stirring, hear my voice getting louder. I was determined to keep my tone even, my words soft. His power might have the ability to make me forget completely. I hadn't tested the limits of it yet and I really didn't want to. I knew very well that if I pushed him, there was a good chance he might just turn up the power and try again.

"Your family is important to you then?" His voice was filled with uncertainty. It was almost like he was a small child, asking for an explanation to something completely beyond his understanding.

"My family is everything to me. They're my heart, my world, my reason for being. Without them..." I shrugged, still unsure of how I could truly explain what my family meant to me. I wasn't even sure there were words to describe the strength of the bond we shared, much less to someone who clearly had never experienced that kind of love themselves.

"You will not leave them, even for such an opportunity as to rule over all of the water this world possesses?"

I shook my head again. "I can't leave them. I wouldn't know how to go on living without them." As something occurred to me, I leaned away from him, tilted my head, working to fill my voice with the confusion I felt very clearly. "Do you not have family of your own?"

He shook his head just a little as he answered. "Not in the way that you seem to." He looked off in the distance—and, somehow I knew he was looking to the closest place where water met land.

It made me wonder. Did he think of the sea as his family—or the creatures that inhabited it... or was he, perhaps, thinking of someone else—maybe someone he had lost. His next words might have answered my question, but they were spoken so matter-of-factly, I couldn't be sure.

"My parents passed on some time ago. I have been searching for my Queen ever since. I had hoped to create a family with my Queen." He looked meaningfully at me again, but didn't press forward—either physically or supernaturally—and I was thankful for it.

The mother within me was feeling his pain, the loss

of his parents, even parents that might have kept themselves somewhat apart from him because of their duty, would be difficult for anyone.

I could not imagine how I would go on if I lost my mother. Which brought me right back to the problem at hand.

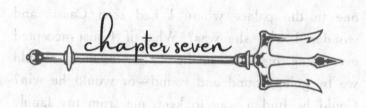

chapter seven

WE STOOD THERE FOR SEVERAL VERY long seconds—or minutes—I really couldn't tell, neither of us saying anything. What was there to say really? I couldn't possibly explain to him how important my family was to me and why I could never just leave them—and he was obviously not giving up on the idea of me coming with him.

Which left us with nothing to say.

The tension between us built, becoming nearly as unbearable as the heat I had been fighting against since I had first bumped into him.

Finally, I couldn't take it anymore. I had to do

something—if only to keep him from trying to force me away again, erasing my memories in the process. I had boldly proclaimed that I could fight him, but deep down I was worried. If he knew I could fight him, he would just work harder to hide those memories from me.

And what if I didn't have another moment like the one in the palace where I had seen Cassie and wondered who she was? What if I just accepted everything this time—or the next or the next? Would we be going round and round—or would he win? Could he find a way to keep me from my family forever?

They knew something about what had happened now—so they wouldn't be in the dark. But there would be nothing they could do. It was pretty obvious the palace he had taken me to was either in the deepest parts of the ocean or so cleverly hidden, no human could ever find it—since no one ever had. So, there was no hope that my family could.

Not that they exactly have the resources to rent the sort of equipment they would need to look for an underwater city...

The thought did not make me feel any better about the whole situation. And, something about his expression told me he knew exactly what I had just been thinking. I don't know how I knew, but I did.

"What?" I said it with sarcasm, but also with determination. I would not give in. He might as well know it right up front.

"I cannot marvel at the way your mind works?" This was said in a tone of awe and respect, but there was an undertone I could hear that told me he was also mocking me—at least a little.

How do I know his tones so well? I barely know the man, but it's like I can read his mind.

And then, there was another thought that answered my own—inside my head, just like my own thoughts.

"Because you can."

I stepped back in shock when I looked up and realized that he had done that. He had somehow put his own thoughts into my head. Was that how he was doing whatever he had been doing to make me feel attracted to him?

Looking at him, I realized I didn't even need to ask. I knew the answer. It was right there in his mind —which, I realized for the first time, I could hear... when I wanted to. What I had thought of as my own thoughts—confirming what I thought or suspected to be true—were actually his. And I was hearing them inside my mind.

Unfortunately, he didn't have to try to make me feel attraction for him. Maybe he did use the charm thing, but somewhere deep inside I knew that I would have been drawn to him, all on my own. Some people believe in love at first sight. I believed that this King and I were meant to be together.

Which would make it all the more difficult to make him understand that I could never choose him over my family...

I moved over to the small alcove of trees beside the house—where Cassie had dragged two chairs so that she could sit under the trees and read—and sat down, hard, in one of the chairs.

Telling myself this could not be real, that it must all be some sort of strange and disturbing dream or a hallucination—and if I ignored it all, everything would go away—was what I wanted to do.

I also knew it wouldn't really help.

But all of the things swirling around in my mind like a crazed out-of-control teacup ride at some ridiculous theme park—his abduction of me, whatever he had done to change me into whatever I was now, the real and outrageous mermaid tail that my daughter wanted... when I absolutely did not... and now the information that this man whom I barely knew could not only read my mind, but put his own thoughts and will into my head, control me with his mind, seduce me without ever saying a word or laying a hand on me, and that he clearly would follow me to the ends of the Earth to do so—was all too much for me to handle.

And, I said as much.

"You know, this is all just too much." I remembered, halfway through my sentence that he probably already knew what I'd been thinking before

I said it—since he could read my mind—but there was something helpful in saying the words anyway. With that in mind, I kept going, still talking out loud even though he was probably reading every word before it could ever actually come out of my mouth.

"I'm not prepared for this sort of thing. I'm just a person. I..." The realization that I wasn't actually still just a person stopped me. Whatever he had done to me had obviously made me in no way *"just a person"* anymore. That made me angry.

I stood quickly, nearly knocking the chair over in my rush to give him the piece of my mind that he certainly deserved.

"How dare you! How could you do this to me... without my permission, without even a warning..." I started to lose steam when I caught sight of his expression. But, a moment later, I caught just a hint of my daughter's face in the window above us. She was looking out, trying to be stealthy about it, but failing in the cutest possible way—and that gave me renewed anger.

"And you took me away from my family. How could you do that to me?" I sank back down into the chair with the next thought—which I didn't voice. I already knew the answer. I didn't even have to read his mind to find it out. I knew—just as well as I knew that, if I continued to fight him, he would just do what he had done already... again.

He would erase my memories and take me back to

his deep sea prison and put me through all that ceremony and nonsense and keep me there forever — and I would truly never see my family again, because I was certain that this time he would keep a better watch on my mind. He would monitor closely to make sure no hint of a whisper of memory would return.

At the thought of it—and, when I looked up at him, his face confirmed my worst fears without needing a nod or a word—I found I could barely breathe for how intense the pain within me became. Every inch of my being felt as if I were breaking open and shattering into a million tiny glass shards... shards he would then break into even smaller pieces with his not caring about what I wanted or knowing how desperately important my family was to me.

"Truly, I had no idea." He didn't push the thoughts into my mind—which was a relief. And he didn't say them in the more than slightly imperious tone he'd been using with me until now either, which gave me hope.

Hope I quickly squashed. The last thing I needed was false hope to be crushed again.

We sat there in silence for what felt like an eternity. Seeing no solution at hand, there was little else I could think to do—and I had run out of things to say.

He said nothing. And while I knew I could have looked into his mind to see what he was thinking, I didn't. He had showed me the courtesy—and deserved it in return. Also, there was the very real possibility that I didn't want to know what he was thinking.

So, in silence we sat. I looked up toward the window after a few minutes, but either my daughter had given up watching or my mother had come and dragged her away. I felt inexplicably lonely in that moment.

Yes, I had dragged him away from my family so that he wouldn't say something unfortunate and entirely unsuitable in front of my young and impressionable daughter, but I hadn't really thought about the fact that I would be facing him all alone, with no one on my side of things—and with no real hope of changing his mind about taking me away from here.

And that was when the answer struck.

I turned toward him, unsure of whether or not he had already seen the thought in my head, but determined to make him see that it was the best way —whatever it took.

"I have a thought."

When he looked up at me, every trace of haughtiness and superiority had been wiped from his features. He looked more like a frightened child than a stubborn and powerful man set on having his way.

"I already know what you are going to say."

When he stopped, looking even more uncertain than he had a moment ago, I realized he had no idea what to say... for maybe the first time in his life. One look at him told me this was an entirely new experience for him. He was accustomed to being in command, to being in control, to being feared and obeyed without question or complaint.

Clearly, whatever he was thinking—and I was tempted for a moment to just reach out and see what it was, but I stopped myself before temptation got the better of me—had him shaken and unsure of everything.

He didn't go on though. He reached forward and pulled me into his arms, half leaning down to close the difference in height between us and half pulling me up against his hard body so that he could kiss me.

This time was different than any other. There was no heat coming from him... except for where his lips met mine, where his hands held me tightly, crushing my shirt in his fists. He was pulling me against him with only his hands and the unexpected explosions of lust that were blooming on my skin everywhere it touched his.

But I felt none of the supernatural tendrils of desire that should have been sneaking through me, pulling me to him, sending thoughts of attachment and duty to make me feel bound to him through my head, and turning the memories of my children and my life to mush and fog.

There was simply body heat and natural desire— though, after a few moments, I did feel that same desperate lack of breath... not because I couldn't get air... more because breathing was becoming more difficult with the intensity of our shared desire.

After what felt like a few seconds... or an eternity, he pulled back slowly, gently, not letting go of me, but removing his lips from mine. It could have been my imagination, but it felt reluctant on his part. A moment later, he actually tightened his grip just a bit —and at the same time, rested his forehead against mine. His lips were no more than a whisper from mine, but he did not kiss me again.

We were both breathing heavily and the air between us was charged with more than our breath.

Neither of us spoke —and, I didn't look, but I had the distinct and intense feeling that he was feeling just as churned up and confused as I was by all of this. How that was possible, I couldn't say... He was the King of the freakin' ocean, for crying out loud!

What... seriously... what could he possibly see in me?

The thought came, but I didn't know if he read it or not. There was no reaction from him —and no answer either. He just stayed where he was, the desire and frustration radiating off of him as strongly as if he were using his supernatural gift —even though I could tell somehow that he wasn't.

When he finally did pull away, I could again feel his reluctance, which perplexed me. Why was he reluctant —and yet, he wasn't using his abilities to bind me to him again?

I wanted to, but I didn't ask—and he didn't answer. So, clearly he wasn't reading my thoughts again. We simply stood there, looking at each other—as if we were both trying to figure out what had happened... and what to say next.

Finally, he let go completely, took a step back.

I had no idea what to expect now. Was he stepping back to get out of the way of the water that was coming to take me away? Was he stepping back to look at me—and then demand I change before we go? Was he...? I didn't get to finish my train of thought because he finally spoke.

"I will be going now." And with that, he started to turn away.

"But..." He turned back at my words, looking almost as if I had slapped him... or stabbed him. "I don't understand."

He sighed, then took a step back toward me. "I am going now. I see that I was wrong to force you to come with me. You will stay here, with your family." He looked away, toward the house—and his expression was almost wistful.

Was he jealous of my family?

"I don't understand. You're going back, but you're not going to make me come with you?" I knew I sounded simple... maybe even a little stupid, but I was genuinely confused. Nothing he'd said just now—and nothing he'd done in the last few minutes made any sense. It didn't line up with his earlier behavior... or attitude... or everything he had said pretty much since I'd met him.

So... why now?

"I understand now. You belong here. I had no right to take you from them—or them from you. I wish I could see another solution, some answer that would give us both what we want, what we need." With that, he looked back at me, shrugging a little, as if to say that he had no clue what to do.

I knew exactly what he meant. After everything that had happened, I was surprised to find myself wishing he could somehow stay—a thought that both confused and somewhat frightened me.

"You know where to find me." He spoke quietly, a tinge of sadness to his voice. And then—before I could say anything or stop him, he was swallowed up in a thick column of water.

I took a step forward, my hand reaching out—for what I didn't know—but it was too late. He was gone before my foot landed.

I stood there for several seconds, just waiting, and watching, turning away only at the sound of running feet.

And then my sweet Cassie was launching herself at me, wrapping her arms around my waist and squeezing with all her strength.

"Mommy, you did it. You sent the bad man away —and you're still here!"

I nodded, still somewhat confused on that

situation, but happy to be home, with my family, and not forced to forget them, and stuck in some faraway place where they could never find me.

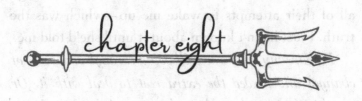

chapter eight

TO SAY THAT LIFE WENT ON AS USUAL would have been nice. But, life did not go on just as it always had. Not for me. Not for my family.

For one thing, I had to track down my car. Even being gone only for a day—the shopping center that housed my favorite coffee house had not just left my car there. They'd had it towed. It was an annoyance I hadn't been prepared for, but in the grand scheme of things—probably the least of my worries. So, I tracked it down, called a cab to take me to where it was, paid the ridiculously exorbitant fees—and then drove home.

For another thing, I had to explain to my boss why I hadn't been at work that day—and the day before, when I'd woken up and everything had gone insane. My mother had called in to work to tell them I was sick so I wouldn't lose my job, but she hadn't known exactly what to say about what was wrong with me. She'd gone with I'd passed out and then slept through all of their attempts to wake me up—which was the truth. I just hadn't known about it until she'd told me.

Perhaps my body was still going through some sort of changes and needed the extra rest to deal with it. Or maybe I had just been through too much for my mind to deal with and it had opted for the oblivion of sleep.

Either way, I had slept through them all trying to wake me. I'd slept through breakfast being cooked and lunch. I'd slept through the sounds of Cassie as she played both in her room and outside. Which meant I'd slept through a countless slamming of the door as she went in and out.

That was all life as usual. And it went on around me as I tried to deal with what I'd been through—and what I would likely be going through for some time to come.

Because, for another thing, I was different. He had made me different. I felt myself being pulled toward he water—and at the oddest times. It was different from the feelings I'd had when he was around—no heat, no charm, just a pull that I fought... mostly because I had no idea what it meant or what would happen if I let it overtake me.

Still... I found myself staring off in the direction of the ocean, distracted from whatever I had been doing at the moment.

I also lived in a near constant state of fear that the tail would come back—and I wouldn't be able to make it go away. Since I hadn't done it before, I could only think that he had somehow made it appear... and then disappear with his own powers.

Powers—it was another thing that frightened me.

When I had begun to remember in the undersea palace, I must have used my abilities to get away from him—and return to my family...but how, I had no idea. And, I was frightened to try and figure it out.

Whatever control I'd had over it all under the ocean—sending the servants away, making him tell me things, somehow transporting myself away from the undersea palace and back to my little house. I didn't seem to have it now.

There was nothing in my mind that told me how I'd done any of it—or how to do it again. There was no instruction manual or thoughts in my mind that answered the millions of questions and concerns I had about what I had done or what I could do. And, most of all—what would happen if I did it again, without meaning to.

When I'd used the transportation ability before, I had been thinking only of getting back to my family. I could only think that my maternal instincts had somehow tapped into the ability to travel using water to bring me back here.

But how to do it without that... and not end up back under the ocean accidentally was the question. A question I was not prepared to answer or deal with the consequences of.

So, I didn't try.

I simply went about my days as normally as I could. I used doors. I drove. I went to work. I did my job as best I could—which fortunately didn't take a lot of concentration. When I had started working as a bank teller, I'd had to focus on my counting. Now, the machines did everything for us. The only counting I ever did was when I happened to be in the lobby—which didn't happen much—instead of the drive through area.

In the lobby, customers liked for us to count the money out to them. In the drive through, it wasn't really possible. So, all I had to do was put what the machine spit out in an envelope and then into the little plastic shell to send out to the customer.

Far too often when I had no customers, I would find myself looking off into the distance, the pull of the sea distracting me from everyone and everything around me.

More than once, one of the other tellers would shake me out of my daze—and I worried about those times. Just how strongly had the pull been to make me completely unaware of what was going on around me?

And, worst of all, when I zoned out so completely, what were the chances that my abilities... that I didn't understand at all... might kick in somehow without my permission and follow that pull? What would I do if that did happen? How could I explain that to anyone?

To disappear in a column of water from inside a bank would be the worst way of outing myself to everyone. At that point, I had a terrible feeling that, if I did manage to find my way back, the government would be waiting to take me off to some secret underground military base where they would poke and prod and experiment on me to find out how I had done it. And the worst part was, I would have no idea how to explain or even show them. Which presented the absolutely terrifying question of how far they would go to force it to happen.

With all of that plaguing me, every minute of every hour of every day, the most pressing thought in my mind was that I would never be able to have a normal life again.

And it was all his fault... a man whose name I didn't even remember... if I had indeed ever known it —a man I had no idea how to find or even contact.

The most frightening part was thinking... if I did somehow figure out how to contact him... Would he take the abilities from me if I asked—or just start pushing me again to join him under the sea?

A part of me wanted to find out. Another part of me really didn't want to know. Neither part had any idea how to try.

One thing was for sure; something had to change... somehow—or I was going to end up a lab rat for the government... or worse.

Although the constant fear made it feel much longer, no more than a week had passed before he showed up again. He was still in a fancy suit, which made me feel ridiculously underdressed—in my jeans and bank logo polo shirt.

When he arrived, I had no idea. I missed his grand entrance. He was just there... standing by my car when I walked out of the bank. I headed toward the parking lot initially with my head down, searching through my purse for the keys that always seemed to find their way to the most remote corner of a bag that should not have been big enough to hide them so well.

When I looked up, halfway to my car—keys in hand—he was there, standing straight and proud by my fifteen year old car that was obviously in need of a good washing. He didn't look at all like he was standing in a bank parking lot by a dirty SUV. He looked like he was in a throne room, preparing to hand down some royal wisdom to his subjects.

It stopped me in my tracks... literally. I stopped moving, right where I was—right there in the middle of the parking lot and just stared.

Whether or not he was emitting that supernatural charm of his, I couldn't be sure—but I couldn't help noticing how good he looked, how well he filled out his suit, his too-handsome features, his obvious strength. The memory of how he had looked in his armor and crown came to mind. My body reacted almost instantly, on full alert of his proximity—even though I tried everything I could think of to block the reaction, reminding myself how high-handed he had been, reminding myself that he had kidnapped me— and removed all memory of my family.

After a minute though, heat was rushing over my skin and every cell in my body reached out psychically toward his, the anger... the annoyance... the frustration—it was like so much smoke... or fog, blowing away in the blinding bright light of whatever this was between us.

And then it stopped—so suddenly, it was as if someone had thrown a bucket of cold water at me.

I stood there, still in the middle of the parking lot, gasping for air as the shock—the sheer intensity of it —flooded over me and robbed me of sense or breath.

And he... he stood there with his head hanging like a small boy who has been caught with his hand in the cookie jar. His dejection and shame was evident in his entire body. His shoulders were slumped forward and inward, as if he were trying to curl into himself and hide.

Not at all unlike something I've seen Dylan do at least a dozen times.

Somehow, the combination of his boyish show of shame and my own sense of fair play sparked just enough forgiveness within me to give him a chance. I started to move toward him... slowly at first, testing the waters so to speak. When I started to move toward him, he was still curled in on himself, so he did not notice. I was within inches of him before he started to raise his head a little and look at me with the most sheepish expression I had seen on his strongly handsome features.

It was all I could do not to giggle at how intensely young and frightened he looked in that moment. With the skills honed fine over my nearly sixteen years of motherhood, I managed to restrain myself.

We stood there just like that for nearly a minute before he spoke—and when he did, my surprise was almost as difficult to contain as my urge to laugh. His voice was vastly different, lacking it's usual forcefulness and assurance, his words were quiet, spoken slowly and carefully. Clearly this was new territory for him—and he was obviously uncertain and uncomfortable.

"My apologies."

When I only nodded, which any human would have known was my way of accepting his apology... but he clearly did not, he went on. "Would it be possible for you to find it within yourself to forgive me?"

And then, before I could even open my mouth to answer, he rushed on "No. I do not deserve forgiveness. I have no excuse for myself. I will go." And just like that, the water swirled around him, appearing at his internal command, to whisk him away.

But this time, I was prepared. I reached out and took hold of his arm, concentrating as hard as I could on keeping him right where he was. I looked deep within myself, to the places I had been actively trying to ignore, and called up the ancient knowledge I hadn't even known was there. I matched wills with the King of the Seas. The water fought me, struggling between his will and mine, unsure of who to obey — until finally, with a level of surprise I could have felt even without our supernatural connection, he released his hold on it.

It disappeared as quickly as it had appeared, leaving him entirely dry, still looking somewhat like the ashamed schoolboy, but also astonished. There were other emotions I could see in his eyes and those handsome features that I was hesitant to identify and then deal with... but they would have to be addressed at some point. Of that, I was strangely certain. His coming here was just further evidence that the situation was not going away....

We stood there for several moments without speaking, even though it felt as if there were whole conversations hanging in the air between us. He was the one who broke the silence.

"I feel as if I have already ruined the reasons I came here."

Unfortunately, I was in no position to listen or acknowledge his statement. My tapping into the ancient knowledge and powers he had somehow given me, came with way too much new information. There were things about him that I did not want to deal with or know about really; an immeasurable library in my head about the man who was responsible for ruling over the Earth's oceans.

With that came everything there was to know about the oceans themselves—and every sort of creature that inhabited them.

Then, there was all of the knowledge about how to use my new abilities, what I could do, even how he had managed to bestow all of these strange new powers upon me; a mere mortal... or, maybe not so much a mere mortal anymore...

I didn't want to to deal with any of it, but my brain wasn't listening to that. It was busy gleefully unpacking everything, laying it all out so that it filled my head with so much that I couldn't even begin to handle it all.

I must have made some sort of face... or else he was reading my thoughts again, because he spoke up, just as he reached out and touched me.

"Are you well?"

I didn't answer. I had no response, no way to speak. I couldn't even think clearly, to find some way to give him a sign that I was not alright, that something was happening to me, something I was not ready for—but my mind was charging ahead regardless.

And then my body took over—and, for the second time since meeting him, I passed out.

chapter nine

WHEN I OPENED MY EYES, MY FIRST thoughts were definitely panic-related. The last time I had lost consciousness with him around, I had woken up at the bottom of the ocean in a sunken shipwreck, somehow able to breathe underwater.

I pushed myself to a sitting position and looked around, more than a little relieved to see that the room I was in looked nothing like a shipwreck—and when I moved, I didn't float off the bed. Still... I was in a bed that was not my own—and he was clearly around somewhere, and all of that worried me more with each passing second.

When he had shown up at my job, I'd been surprised, but also strangely happy to see him—and without any use of his supernatural charm ability to influence me. Then he had tried to run away...

At the very thought of it, I winced... expecting pain to come rushing in again—or, at the very least, confusion and an overwhelming info dump. But nothing happened. Whatever my mind had opened up by tapping into my new abilities had either been dealt with... or had he done something?

Was that why I was here now, in this room? Had he done something to stop the madness that had been swirling around inside my head? And why here? Why not somewhere underwater? It wasn't as if I couldn't breathe there—or leave there if it got to be too much for me?

Or...had he brought me here out of respect for my desire not to be underwater... so far away from my family? I looked around again, paying more attention to the room itself—now that I knew I was not in some strange underwater sunken ship... or in his palace... without my memories.

It was a very nice room, a hotel room maybe—or possibly a bedroom in an apartment. Which made me wonder, had he rented an apartment nearby—or gotten a hotel room?

Why would he do that?

There were no answers, nothing in the room to tell me specifically either way, and no echoes of thoughts to tell me what I wanted to know.

And that realization stopped my searching around the room. I couldn't hear his thoughts. I wasn't being assaulted by the mind-crushing weight of a millennia's worth of information about the ocean and everything in it.

Why?

Had he somehow taken the abilities from me? Had he decided to let go gracefully—and he'd needed to bring me here to do whatever was necessary to undo what had been done underwater last time?

Was that why I was not underwater—because I could no longer breathe underwater?

I pushed myself off the bed...ready to dance around the room in excitement, only to stop—when I realized that I could hear his thoughts... from the next room.

I dropped back down onto the bed with a heavy sigh—just as the door opened and he walked into the room.

His expression was very much like it had been, a little boy in trouble. Clearly, he had been listening in on my thoughts—and heard my excitement... and then my intense disappointment.

Perhaps he had been shielding his thoughts from me until then—and he'd let me back in before I could get too excited. When I realized that he was nodding —answering the question in my thoughts without intruding too much, I felt like screaming.

This entire situation is ridiculously unfair—you

know that, right? Tell me you know that! I sent the thoughts at him like daggers, sharpening my internal tone as much as I could, determined to ram the message home one way or another.

I have a life. I have two children who need me. I have a mother looking to me to take care of her, now that she's retired. I do not have time for this nonsense.

The sadness on his features only deepened. His whole demeanor changed with it. He curled in on himself like he had before, making me feel like the worst person in the entire world.

It was then that I realized, all of the information that had assaulted me before was still there in my mind. Just thinking of his responsibilities made me aware of them. I could see the information in my head like words flashing across a computer screen. From his duties to his people to everything he was responsible for in all of the seas across the world. And when I focused my thoughts on his family, his lineage, that information came to the surface of my mind.

It was all easily accessible though—no bombardment, no barrage, no mind-crushing weight of information that was too much for my fragile human mind.

So, whatever he'd brought me here for was to my benefit... obviously. It just wasn't what I had been hoping for—which, again, made me feel like the worst person ever. It must have been quite a shock to him, in the next room to give me privacy, shielding his thoughts from me so I would not be overwhelmed again—and here I was celebrating... probably making him feel terrible in the process.

"You worry too much. The truth could not make me feel terrible."

It was a little bit surprising that he spoke aloud, but what was one more surprise in what had already been a day of surprises and shocks—nearly as many as the day I had met him. Before I could answer, he went on.

"I only wish that I could give you what you want."

There it was—the bombshell I had been waiting for, the end result of all of this. So, there was no reversing whatever he had done to me.

As I thought it—I noticed him shaking his head slowly. Again, he was answering my thoughts and giving me privacy at the same time. If I had not been so annoyed by the whole thing, it would have seemed sweet. I was sure of it. But I was annoyed by the whole thing. It was ridiculously annoying.

I'd been taken against my will, changed into some freak.

He made a noise that must have been in reaction to my last thought, and I tried to look apologetic, but could not get my face to agree.

So, I spoke instead. "I am sorry. I truly don't mean to insult you. I cannot help that my human mind goes right to that word when I think of all the weird things that have happened to me. For me, having a mermaid tail appear randomly—and somehow make me naked in the process—is just weird and freaky." I stopped a moment, waving at the sudden heat in my cheeks.

When I looked over to where he stood, I could see he was having a reaction to my words as well, but he looked surprised by it, which must mean he had nothing to do with mine.

I walked over to where he stood and took his hand in mine before I went on. "I am sorry if I'm saying this all wrong." I shrugged—and then kept going. "I don't exactly know how to deal with all of this."

He smiled, and reached up with his other hand to wrap it around mine. "I see that now." He looked down before going on. "I hope you will forgive me. I did not see that before. I should have spoken with you, explained, given you more of a chance to speak up for what you wanted."

There was still one thing he hadn't answered out loud... though he sort of had already with the shaking of his head. Some part of me just had to hear it spoken out loud.

"So, then, I'm stuck like this? There's no changing me back, is there?"

He shook his head again but must have also heard in my thoughts how important it was for me to hear him say the words.

"There is no reversing what has been done. Once the gift has been bestowed, it is forever a part of you. There is no going back."

I stumbled backwards a little, but his strong arms came around me, kept me from falling or losing my balance. He held me for another moment, making certain I was steady. Then he started to let go.

I didn't let him.

I reached up and wrapped my arms around his waist, curling my fingers around the fabric of his jacket, pulling myself even closer. Then I leaned against his strong chest, needing that strength more than I would have... could have... ever imagined.

The intensity of what he'd just told me weighed down on me, pressing into me. I felt as if I would break apart, into a million tiny little pieces any second now.

I would never just be me again.

No matter if I went with him under the ocean — or I stayed here with my family, I would never just be the me I had grown up to be. I was forever changed. I could never go back to being normal. I could never stop these strange things from happening, these abilities I barely understood. They would continue to overwhelm me... forever.

The weight of it was nearly too much. How would I go on? How could I live my life? Be normal... pretend to be normal? The answer was simple and yet I didn't want to deal with it. I couldn't deal with it yet. And so I clung to him, holding so tightly, my fingers started to go numb.

If only I could find a way to rewind time, to go

back to that day when this had all started and stop myself from going into the store, meeting him, starting this insane chain reaction that had forever altered me...

"It would not have changed anything." His voice was very quiet, but being wrapped so tightly against him, it was like a megaphone in my ears.

Or maybe it was just what he'd said. Shock had me letting go, stepping back, looking up at him in surprise and denial. That couldn't be right—could it? Nothing I had done that day would have changed this outcome? How was that even possible?

"I was sent to find you."

I put a hand up as he started to move toward me. "No. Wait. What? Sent to find someone... or to find me specifically?" I stepped back, determined to put some distance between us now.

He stepped back too, took a breath before answering.

"Sent to find you specifically. Only you." I started to argue, to protest, something... but he went on.

"It was foretold, seen by our most respected elders. They sent me to you, told me you were willing. I didn't know it then, but they had been watching you for some time."

I stumbled backward at that, ramming solidly into a very thick, hard, heavy piece of furniture at my back —which stopped my movement, but did nothing to curb my incredulity at his words.

"I don't understand."

He nodded, then quietly went on. "This is the way it has always been when the royal Prince has difficulty finding his own mate."

"Mate?" The way the words tasted in my mouth made me want to spit them out, but I worked to soften them at least.

"Yes. I know it is not a word your people care for, but it is the best description our people have for what we seek. A mate of the heart, of the mind, of the body, and the soul. We search for someone who will spend the rest of their days with us, someone who will be a perfect match for us."

I let out a short bark of laughter at those words. He stopped for a moment, his lips turned up in what could only be called an ironic smile, and then went on.

"It did seem strange to me that my one true match would be a land dweller. However, I trust the elders. They have never steered me wrong before."

"Never?" I didn't really mean to ask—and I knew he could have read the question in my mind anyway, but the word was out before I could stop it.

He was already nodding in answer. "Never. I have trusted them on so many things in my life already."

"Doesn't seem like it really worked out this time around though." Again, the words tripped out of my mouth before I really knew what I was saying. They might be true, but I normally wasn't cruel. I shook my head a little at the peculiarity of my own behavior.

Yes, I was angry, but was I trying to hurt him? And, if yes, why?

He was looking down at the floor again as he spoke, the small boy swamped with shame had returned. "It is understandable, how you feel."

I started to argue, but he interrupted. "No. It is. I tried to take you from your home, your life, your family. You should be angry."

When I started to speak again, he went on. "I would be angry if someone had done such a thing to me." And he meant it. I could feel that all the way to my toes. He meant every word he was saying.

"Why did you come today?" I had no idea where the question had come from, but it felt so right, I didn't let myself hesitate. I pushed ahead quickly. Wanting to take him by surprise. "I'm not talking about right now, bringing me here—or when you came into the room a few minutes ago. I mean earlier."

When he said nothing, just stood there looking as if I had knocked the air out of him, I kept going. "Why did you show up so unexpectedly... at my job... without using any of your abilities on me."

He still said nothing. Just stood there, staring at me. "You could have. You have to know that." And I took a step forward, braver than I had felt in a very long time. "I was exhausted. It was a long day of me holding tight to the abilities you gave me, trying not to splash someone with water because they were a jerk."

I was standing right in front of him now. "I was absolutely worn out." I reached up and put a hand on his chest. "You could have taken me right back."

This time he took a step back. I moved with him. "I probably wouldn't have even noticed until it was too late." I kept the hand on his chest, even as he took another step back. "We could be there right now."

I was surprised at how I sounded—and at how invigorated I suddenly felt. Where there had been exhaustion, there was now a boundless amount of energy. I felt as if I could run a marathon and still be full of energy. I was curious as to why, but I was still much more interested in the effect I was having on the regal, imposing, intimidating Sea King.

When his back hit the wall behind him, he had no choice but to stop. I did not. I stepped forward until I was leaning into him. Not for balance or reassurance. Not this time. No, this time I was thoroughly enjoying throwing him off balance.

I was enjoying the moment, but I was still a little bit surprised at my own voice as I said. "I'm not making you nervous, am I?" My voice was more self-assured than I would have expected from myself. "Not little ol' me." And there was something about the tone of my voice that surprised me more than a little.

He wasn't using his charm on me. That was obvious. I wasn't trying to use mine on him, but still... something about the way my voice kept saying the words brought to mind a dark room somewhere, tangled limbs and sweaty sheets.

When that image popped into my mind—in far more clarity and detail than I was comfortable with, he stopped retreating. His mouth came down on mine, not hard, not crushing, but with an intensity that was unsettling.

Not that I was thinking about that too much in the moment.

As he wrapped his arms around me, lifting me right off my feet, I reached up, tangling my fingers in his hair. I wanted him closer. I wanted us closer. I wanted...

He stopped, set me on my feet—and, as I stumbled back a little, he moved out from between me and the wall, turning me with him as he held only tightly enough to make sure I didn't fall.

It took several very long seconds to regain my balance. My legs felt like jelly... or water, really really soft water. They didn't want to hold me up, as I stood there trying to catch my breath and figure out just what exactly had happened in this room a minute ago... and a few seconds ago.

Had I really chased him across the room, becoming the aggressor somehow? Had I really succeeded in making him so uncomfortable that his only choice was escape?

And then, when I had unwittingly dragged him into my desire, he'd given in. But then... for what reason I could not imagine, he had also put a stop to it.

Which brought me right back to my question.

"Why did you come here today?" This time the words were spoken softly, shakily, as if I had no control over my own voice.

He didn't let me go, but he had already put as much distance between us as he could without letting me fall.

"I don't know." When he looked up at me, his expression was unreadable—and his voice held a note of uncertainty that somehow made me feel both better and worse about the whole situation.

He had come to see me, likely with some sort of idea to make peace with me over what had all happened. When I had passed out on him, he had been a perfect gentlemen. He had not taken me back under the ocean again without telling me.

And now I had him second guessing himself and feeling uncertain about things he shouldn't.

But... a small voice in the very back of my mind found an argument I was not at all comfortable with... *at least you've proved to yourself that you can take him on and come out on top.*

I shook my head to dispel those thoughts. I did not want to win that way. I really didn't want to win at all. I didn't want to play. I was dragged into the game against my will—and I just wanted out.

I was pulled from my internal debate by the touch of his hand. While I had been busy arguing with myself, whether he had been listening in or not, he had moved forward and reached out, taking my hand in his... probably for no other reason than to get my attention.

I looked down at that hand—and then back to his handsome face. His expression now was readable. But I was not at all certain I wanted to know what he was thinking.

Because what I was thinking was that my body had overplayed my hand...

He surprised me then by laughing, loud and full. He laughed for several seconds, almost long enough to make me uncomfortable—before he spoke... explained.

"Do you know, I do not even need to read your mind to see precisely what you are thinking?

Overplayed my hand indeed. He was just messing with me.

Now I was annoyed. Before I could pull free, he tightened his hold on my hand, stepped closer. "It is most refreshing."

"Don't you mean amusing!" I snapped. Embarrassed more than I wanted to admit, I looked away. I tried to focus on anything else in the room, but mostly I was just determined to look anywhere but at him.

He moved around, so that he was in front of my searching gaze. Childishly, I looked back the other direction.

He didn't step again. Instead, he reached up and gently took hold of my face, moving my head so that I was forced to look at him.

I blew out a breath and waited. I knew I could have just looked away without turning my head again. I could have yanked my face out of his light grip. I could have stepped back, turned and left the room, used a column of water to disappear. But all of those things felt incredibly immature—and I wanted to be an adult about all of this. Or at least try to.

I blinked once, cleared my throat, and stood my ground. He didn't stop smiling, but he did drop the hand that had been holding my face—and he kept a loose hold of my hand, but took a small step back as well.

"I believe I know the answer to your question." He was still smiling.

"What question?" I was still trying really hard not to be annoyed... and to be adult about the whole situation, so I wasn't really thinking about what question I had asked—twice now.

"Why I came today." Something in his eyes made me feel as if the temperature in the room had doubled. He didn't move closer, but somehow he felt closer. And, I was very certain he was not using that supernatural charm of his, but that didn't stop my skin from heating up... or my body from instinctively leaning in toward him.

I tried to keep my wits about me. "Why?"

"This." He brushed a thumb over the back of my hand—and little sparks of heat spread from the contact point, ran up my arm, rushed across my chest, filling me to my core with a racing, molten lava flow of desire. "You."

He did nothing else. Just slowly brushed his thumb across the back of my hand. My brain tried to process what he had said, but my head was filled with a fog of desire that was blocking any sort of rational thought.

All I could do was murmur an "mmm... hmm..." as he set my skin aflame.

And then he let go. Stepped back. It was almost like someone had thrown a bucket of ice water over me. I stumbled a little—and, this time he did not catch me. He stayed right where he was.

"We have to stop this." There was no small amount of regret and frustration in his voice when he said those words, but there was something else too. A ring of determination that told me that he was committed to what he was saying. There was something he wanted—and he was willing to do whatever was needed to get it.

He said nothing else though, so I asked. "Stop what exactly?" Rational thought had returned—and with it the annoyance I had felt so strongly before. I had an idea of what he meant, but I wanted to hear him say it.

"We have to stop allowing the heat between us to

overwhelm our own good sense."

There it was. It was what I'd thought, but I really had not expected him to actually say the words. Now that he had, I could only applaud him internally. Somehow I had gotten to him—at least a little bit. He was thinking about more than just getting what he wanted on a physical level... or by taking the easy way.

"I agree." I said the words gently, but firmly. I wasn't about to back down—now that I sort of had him where I'd wanted him all along, but there was no need to gloat.

"So, what do we do?" He sounded so normal all of a sudden, like any other man in a situation he had no idea how to get out of. He was in unfamiliar territory and obviously didn't care for it one bit.

I started to answer, if for no other reason than to put him out of his obvious misery. But it only took a moment for me to realize I didn't have the answer. This situation was completely out of my wheelhouse as well.

My marriage had been a mutual attraction of two people who were much too young to have any control over their emotions or hormones. We had stayed together long enough to have two of the most exceptional children on the planet, but by the time our daughter had arrived, we were no longer friends... much less attracted to each other anymore.

We had tried for a time, more for the children than

ourselves, but there had been nothing to build on beyond attraction. We had nothing in common—and becoming parents had only made that more obvious.

In the end, I answered truthfully. "I don't know."

He laughed when I said it—and I figured I must look about as comically miserable as he did.

"Quite a pair, aren't we? A Sea King who's barely spent any time with humans and a landlocked human who has no idea what to do with a King from under the sea."

He laughed again, looking at me with another of his unreadable expressions. I could have looked into his thoughts, but if his desire was as dominant and intense as mine, it would only make things that much more difficult for both of us—so, I stayed out of his head.

We stood there for what felt like a very long time, just staring at each other—both of us waiting for the other to say something.

And then we both spoke at once. "Perhaps we..." "I think..."

It was one of those moments that really makes or breaks the tension in the room—and in our case, it broke it.

And it broke with more intensity than we had been holding back. We rushed together, our lips meeting just as feverishly as they had earlier, any ideas about restraint washed away by the waves of desire that swamped us both.

There was no invading of anyone's mind. Ours were—in that moment—one. Our jumbled thoughts mixed and tumbled together, flowing and crashing into and over each other.

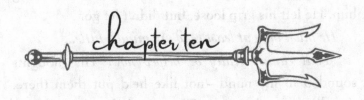

chapter ten

I MAY NEVER KNOW WHAT WOKE ME... some inner clock—or my conscience catching up to me. But the first thing I noticed when I woke, was how tightly we were snuggled together. His arm was wrapped around my waist, pulling me tight up against him and one of my legs was tangled between his.

There would be no quietly sneaking out of this bed or this room, trying to pretend this hadn't happened.

And... before I could try, his hold on me tightened —telling me he must have been awake already.

Nope. No sneaking out for me.

I tried pulling away again, but his arm was like

iron holding me in place. So I shifted instead, wiggling, trying to push against him just enough so that I could turn over. Either he read my mind or figured out what I was doing from my movements because he loosened his grip just enough for me to manage it.

I wiggled and rolled and shifted until I was facing him. He left his grip loose, but didn't let go.

He must have at least read my mind a little...

"That cannot really be helped now." His thoughts sounded in my mind—not like he'd put them there. Just like one of my own. That worried me.

"Wait. You mean... after what..." the words were tumbling out of me, falling over each other in my panic. "... that... somehow linked our thoughts even more than they were before."

He didn't even need to answer out loud. I could hear it in his thoughts. I could see it in his eyes. I could feel it in the tightness of his smile. *I wanted to ask what that was all about, but something more pressing came out first.*

"So, what happened here last night... it's different for you than it is for humans? It affects you differently?"

Great. Yeah. Just my luck. He charms me into bed with his stupid power and them I'm stuck with his voice in my head forever.

I wanted to appreciate that he answered the way I had, without putting his thoughts into my head, but there was too much negativity fighting with the tiny spot of grateful for that.

"It will affect you differently as well. You are more Sea Queen than Human now." I started to speak, but stopped at the tone of his answer. There was something in his voice I was not expecting. And I was surprised to see that he looked almost ashamed at his answer. I could hear it in his thoughts now too. He was genuinely sorry to have done this to me without my consent.

But I could also hear the truth of what he'd told me the evening before. There was literally nothing he could do to take it back. This was a permanent change.

There was no going back.

The question now became, how would we move forward? I couldn't just waste what he had done.

Could I?

"I enjoy watching you think." His voice was low and husky and full of more than just desire. His words though, threw me off a little.

"You what?"

"When you are thinking, especially when it is something of great importance, your face changes. There are tiny lines which appear..." He reached up with the arm that had been holding me tightly to trace along the tiny lines he saw between my eyes with his finger. "... here. I like them."

I wanted to be annoyed that he was trying to

distract me. That had to be what he was doing—right? Nothing else made sense in the moment. I wanted to deny what he was saying... all of it, but somehow I knew that he was right. It was different now.

Before we had been together, I had thought there was a strong attraction between us. But now, just the gentle brushing of his fingers against my skin was almost too much for me to bear—and there was a more intense desire welling up within me, something with a strength of possession I wasn't certain I had the ability to deny.

Instead, I took advantage of the fact that he'd temporarily let go of me. I clamped down hard on the feelings rushing through my body. I pushed away any thoughts of reaching for him or snuggling back up to him. I rolled, quickly, over to the edge and then off the bed.

When my feet hit the floor, I turned back to where he still lay, an odd expression on his handsome face. The new bond between us had his thoughts crowding in on me almost immediately. Hurt, Surprise. Loneliness. They all washed over me like storm waves, slamming into me like the ocean battered a shore.

Then there were my own emotions to deal with. There was such an intense longing to jump back onto the bed—to be as close to him as possible, as soon as possible. It felt like every cell in my body was reaching out to him. I very nearly complied without even thinking.

But then he stopped me... somehow.

"I have had these abilities my entire life. This depth of emotion and attachment, it is nothing new."

"Wait. This is why you're so attached to your people? You feel this way about all of them?"

He laughed out loud at that. Then, answered out loud, as he slid out from under the covers. "Not precisely this way, but you understand now."

He turned his back then, reaching down to the floor—and a moment later, he stood, pulling his pants on as he did so.

I took the cue to look around for my jeans and the polo shirt I'd had on the day before. He stopped me.

"I have fresh clothing for you... if you like."

I stopped, turned, holding the clothing I'd gathered up against me like some sort of shield. As if he hadn't already seen me... all of me—and I could hide behind the wadded up ball of wrinkled clothes.

His next words were out loud again—and I found myself wondering if he even realized he was going back and forth from speaking aloud and communicating with me telepathically.

"I wanted to be prepared..." His voice trailed off at the end, and I found myself pressing against his thoughts... wondering what exactly he was not saying.

The only answers I could get were a sense of embarrassment. Which made no sense to me—but, either he'd figured out how to shut me out of some of his thoughts and feelings or he was working to suppress them. What he'd said earlier about dealing with his abilities all his life came back to me—and I decided to let it go... for now at least.

As I crossed the room to where he stood, he opened what I had not even noticed before, but could see was a large door to a closet that spanned nearly the entire wall it occupied. It was not full by any means, but there were quite a few outfits hanging there. There were dresses, evening gowns, pants, shirts, shoes. It was a veritable treasure trove—and when I stepped closer, I could see one of the dresses that was hung on a special rod that was facing out, I could see that it was my size. That realization filled me with a very strange combination of gratitude and desire and even though I tried very hard to clamp down on the physical reaction my own body had to those emotions, I was unsuccessful.

I turned and threw myself at him, tumbling with him to the floor with him. I was so caught up, I barely noticed the whoosh of sea water around us—and then we were back on the bed.

When I felt myself starting to drift off in his arms again, I pushed myself into a sitting position, pulling out of his loose grip before he had a chance to hold on more tightly and keep me there. I was not at all certain of myself or my capacity for resisting him... especially now. So, I kept going, moving quickly off of the bed, gathering up my discarded clothes, and — careful to keep my gaze away from the large closet — I headed for the other side of the room.

I knew this cycle of giving in to the intense pull between us had to stop. I wasn't at all certain how to make it stop, but I knew that staying close to him was not the way.

There were just too many things that could trigger that deeply intense lust between us.

Because it has to just be lust, right?

I told myself it couldn't be anything else. We barely knew anything about each other — and life had certainly taught me that there was no such thing as love at first sight. Certainly not between someone like him and someone like me.

I was an average looking, overweight, mother of two with a crappy job who lived with her mother and there was absolutely nothing special about me that could possibly interest a man who literally controlled the oceans...

All of them.

And given how much of Earth is covered in ocean, that kinda means he rules the world. Another thought that did not comfort me. He ruled the majority of the space on our world. He was ridiculously handsome. He had muscles for days. And... he had supernatural abilities. Why... how... could he possibly have even the slightest bit of interest in me?

I had pulled my clothes on in such a hurry, the thoughts and worries tumbling end over end through my head the entire time. Now, I took a moment to look in the side mirror over the double sinks in his enormous bathroom.

As I stood there, looking at myself in the mirror, trying to figure out what he could possibly be attracted to, he walked into the room behind me. The moment... the very moment I saw him in the mirror behind me, the desire sprang fully to life and threatened to overwhelm me. Again.

He stepped forward and rested his hands on my shoulders gently, closing his eyes and breathing deeply.

After a moment, I felt the desire begin to ebb... just slightly, just enough for me to take control of it. I breathed a sigh of relief then.

"How do you do that?" The words whooshed out on my exhale, sounding a lot more exhausted and annoyed than I intended.

If he noticed, he didn't comment on it. He only smiled and answered my question. "From birth, remember? Your control will come in time. You need only to learn." After a moment, he added. "I will teach you."

I wanted to be annoyed that he was finding a way to stay connected... to stay a part of my life, but I couldn't. There was no denying the connection we had—and the fact that I was stuck this way. Someone would have to teach me how to control the strange powers I had never asked for. If I was stuck with them... and stuck with this connection I had with him, why shouldn't he be the one to teach me?

I clamped down on the desire that grew from the reminder that he was near... the idea that if he was nearby, teaching me, I could be close to him in other ways too. The imagery that went along with those thoughts were no longer just my imagination—and still... far too appealing.

He must have read my mind—or felt my desire somehow because he did his thing and calmed my desire for him... again. And again, I wanted to be frustrated, but I had to be a little bit grateful that he was helping me to resist—and not just taking advantage of the fact that I now wanted to just crawl back in the bed and have my way with him again... and then let him have his way with me again until neither of us had any strength left.

His hands, still resting gently on my shoulders, squeezed lightly for just a moment before he let go and stepped back. It did not help me to calm the desire, but he was still doing that for me. I looked back into the mirror and saw that he was looking right at me. There were so many things unsaid in his expression. I knew what they were because our minds were so firmly linked now, but seeing the expression of longing—even while he was helping me to calm my own desire—made me realize that I just might have misjudged him about this whole situation.

Yes, technically he had kidnapped me, but he obviously had not done it to take advantage of me. He'd been convinced I would be happy to come live under the ocean with him and his people. He had thought he'd been bestowing this amazing gift to me, something that many other girls... maybe millions of other girls... would have swooned over.

"Why me?" The words were out before I could stop them. I wanted to run from the room, hide somewhere very far away, somehow take back the words, but I was trapped between the wide bathroom counter and him. His muscular body was filling the doorway so that there would be no way I could duck around him.

To his credit, he did not laugh. He didn't even smile. He actually looked slightly annoyed as he stepped forward and reached a hand up toward my face.

"You do not see yourself very clearly, do you?"

His answer plus the soft caress of his hand on my face was enough to knock me completely off balance. He hadn't really answered me, but there was something in the intensity of his eyes and the touch of his hand that told me this was his way of answering.

And then he stepped back, dropping his hand as he did so—and the sudden absence of his touch and the emotions I had been feeling from him just a moment before was like someone had thrown a bucket of ice water on me. I literally gasped at the shock of it. And then I stood there, concentrating on breathing—while he moved away, retreating into the bedroom.

He walked over to the side of the bed, leaned over to pick up his discarded clothing—and I had to force myself to look away. I knew... somehow... that if I watched him getting dressed, I would lose any grip on the tiny amount of self control that I had managed to gather up since he'd stopped helping me and walked away.

When I heard a noise from his general direction—somewhere between a huff and a snort—I figured he'd noticed that I'd looked away and was, for some reason, annoyed by it.

However, a moment later—when the water whooshed over me and the clothes I had just put back on appeared on the foot of the bed that was still quite rumpled—I was the one who became annoyed. I turned away, covering myself with my hands—only to find that I was fully clothed.

Looking down at the clothes I was now wearing, I was more than a little confused. The only thing I could think was that he must have whooshed me into them with his abilities. Why, I had no idea—but it was the only explanation that made sense. I was definitely wearing a different outfit than I had a few moments before... an outfit I had not put on myself. And I had certainly felt the water swirl around me. Since I knew I hadn't done it, it must have been him.

But why?

"Because you do not see yourself clearly." His voice inside my head was gruff, but in the strangest way... cute, at the same time.

I laughed as I turned back toward him. "You know, you've said that to me before. I still don't know what you mean when you say it. Maybe you could explain."

He took a step forward, but then stopped. Then he stepped back. When he spoke, it was much like his mental voice had been... gruff, but cute at the same time.

"You stand there thinking you do not affect me the same way that I affect you. You think you are not attractive or desirable, but you are both—and now that I have..." He said nothing for several moments—and no thoughts were getting through either... just confusion. I could only guess he was searching for the word he wanted.

Finally, he went on "... connected with you..." He accompanied this with a very meaningful look—one that had me blushing. I knew exactly what he meant now.

"You understand?"

I nodded, but found that I couldn't even form a coherent answer in thought form.

"I did not expect to feel this way. I did not expect to be affected this way. I find that even I am having difficulty resisting the pull I feel toward you." His tone sounded less gruff now—more pouty and frustrated. It nearly made me smile, which helped me not be too affected by what he had said.

I had started to feel the heat and the pull as he spoke—almost as if our own abilities were working together against us, pulling us in when we wanted... needed to back away for a bit.

Something about it was definitely different now. He was right about that. He was also correct that it was so much stronger than it had been before. But, somehow this time I was stronger too.

I pushed down against the desire and the heat and I stepped away from him. If I was affecting him the way he affected me, I would remove the temptation.

"Maybe I should go." I took another step toward the door, toward escape."

"When can I see you again?" His voice was no longer pouty or frustrated. It was full of the heat again, a different sort of gruff. The sound of it sent shivers dancing across my skin.

I stubbornly held my ground though... not physically exactly... "I don't know. I think we need some distance right now."

He was moving across the room now, not exactly

stalking me, but there was definitely a hungry look in his eyes.

"This is not a good idea." I took another step back.

He stepped forward. I moved back. I was more than a little nervous now. I had managed to rein in my desire, but he clearly had not—and he still had a much better control over his abilities than I probably ever would. Plus, somewhere deep down, I knew if he got too close... took hold of me... kissed me... I would be lost. I could only hold out for so long against a pull as strong as the ocean's waves.

I could feel them, the waves. They were pulling at me, pushing at me, threatening to knock me down. I needed something strong to hold onto, someone strong. He would protect me. He would keep me from drowning.

And then I was in his arms and he was kissing me again—and I was drowning, but in a completely different way. Those waves were definitely dragging me down, deep and far away from everything else and everyone else.

And that stopped me. The realization that he was once again—whether he meant to or not—making me forget all about my family.

I opened my eyes and, through the water swirling madly around us, I could only see more water. Deep ocean, so far down there was no light from the surface.

I wrenched myself out of his arms and pictured as

firmly and clearly in my mind as I could, my car. And then the water whooshed differently around me—and then I was walking toward my car.

chapter eleven

FORTUNATELY, THE PARKING LOT WAS empty otherwise — and I was parked in the back of the bank, not the front, where I would have been perfectly visible in all my water show glory to the main road and anyone on it.

It was when I put my hand in my pocket out of pure habit that I realized I didn't have my keys. They were in the pants I had left crumpled on a bed in his hotel room. I didn't have my purse or ID either — which wouldn't stop me from driving home. The keys would.

So, I closed my eyes, concentrated on the clothes I

had been wearing, the left pocket of the pants and the keys within. If he could change my clothes completely with his whooshy watery power, I could certainly retrieve a few keys.

When I felt the water swirl over my open palm — and then felt the cold metal of what had to be my keys laying there, I opened my eyes and looked down.

"I did it! I can't believe it. I did it!" Somewhere, a dog barked. And the sound of a car on the road in front of the bank reminded me I might be alone, but I was still out on the open, shouting about something that would make the government agents who just loved to dress in black and skulk around with their badges and total lack of a sense of humor or understanding of personal freedoms just drool to get their hands on it.

So, I clicked the remote with my keys, unlocked my car, got in, put the key in the ignition, started the car, put it in reverse, and started to back out.

And then I slammed down hard on the brakes. Right behind my car, frighteningly close, stood the Sea King himself — fully dressed, looking more than a little annoyed, and holding up my purse where I could see it.

Clearly, I wasn't going to get away from him so easily. With a huff of annoyance, I put the car in park, turned it off, and rolled down my window.

I very specifically did not get out.

I knew it wouldn't make much difference,

ultimately, if he wanted to transport me somewhere again. He would find a way, no matter how many obstacles I put in his way. But, I was not going to make it easy for him. I was going to do everything in my power to keep some control over the situation. Which meant staying in my car.

When he didn't move, but simply continued standing there, I wondered at it. What game was he playing now?

I knew he'd been about to take me back under the ocean. He'd been helping me rein in my now overwhelming desire—and then he hadn't. And when I had mentioned needing some distance, he'd stopped reining anything in—and I just knew we had been headed for his undersea kingdom that last time he'd started to transport us.

Now he was here with my purse, which I obviously would not need under the ocean. Was he using it as a trick to get me close again, so he could pull me with him under the sea—or was he, in his own strange way, possibly apologizing?

I reached out tentatively with my mind, trying to reach his thoughts, trying to figure out what was driving his actions. It seemed like it was what I had thought. It felt sincere.

So, why is there this niggling doubt bothering me? Was it my own inability to resist him? Was it something else?

"I promise. I will behave myself. And I will help you

to behave as well." The thought came into my mind like it had before —more like one of my own thoughts than his —and I found myself stifling a laugh at his phrasing. Though it really wasn't anything to laugh over. It was absolutely on point. I did need help controlling myself.

Only the thought of being pulled away from my family again —and possibly being made to forget them again had made me stop what we were doing and get as far away as possible from him.

Slowly, I reached for the handle on my door. Just giving in to him made the desire rush in, followed quickly by a feeling of control that must be, at least in part, coming from him.

Before I could get out of the car, there was a whoosh of water beside me —and when I looked to see what was going on, I saw my purse sitting on the passenger seat, completely dry of course. I laughed again. Was this his way of telling me he wasn't going to stop me from leaving... he just wanted the chance to speak to me before I did?

I looked into the rearview mirror again. He was still standing behind the car. So, obviously, he still wanted me to get out and talk to him.

But could I risk it? There was no one else around. What would stop him from whooshing me away, leaving my car here with my purse inside, dragging me off to his undersea kingdom and somehow taking all of my memories away again?

The anger that washed over me suddenly must have been his. It swamped me with such an intensity that I gasped in shock and nearly fell out of the car instead of stepping out calmly.

He was there before I could hit the ground, catching me in those strong arms and then stepping back with a huff and a stiffening of those broad shoulders.

"I didn't mean..." I started, but he stopped me with a look.

"You did—and it is my own doing. My anger is with myself. I have not done any of this in the proper way." He stopped there for a moment, but the thoughts rushing through my mind told me enough of what he was trying to convey.

He hadn't spent enough time with people on the surface to understand our ways. He had been pushed into this situation before he was ready to deal with it. His people were still reeling from the aftereffects of the war that had taken his parents lives. He had not expected to have the reaction to me he'd felt from the very first moment—a thought which still confused me. Was it possible he had felt some sort of love at first sight when he'd met me? Was that something different about his people? Had he somehow been attached to me before he'd even made the changes to my body that made me his Sea Queen?

None of it made a bit of sense.

He, was nodding stiffly. "You see. I can apologize,

but it would make little difference. I cannot change what has happened. I cannot take it back. I cannot leave you to your life and go back to mine. We are bound and we are connected and we must find a way to make our peace with it and do what must be done. Together." There was a definite tone of sadness in his voice as he said it, which only confused me more.

Why would he be sad about being connected? Or... and the next thought made much more sense... was he sad about my reluctance to be his Sea Queen, go under the ocean with him, and do whatever it was he wanted me to do?

His thoughts answered me before I could ask out loud—and the feelings of his that washed over me in that moment brought out the woman scorned inside of me. I had been in this position before... well, sort of.

"You know I don't deserve this."

He started to speak, but I rushed ahead, stopping him cold. "My life was going along just fine, thank you. Maybe it doesn't seem really great to someone who rules over all the seas, but it was my life and I was free to live it the way I wanted."

He started to speak again, but I kept going. "I was happy..." The last word came out on a sob—not just because I was mourning the life that I'd had, not just because he had taken all of that from me, not just because I knew things would never be the same again... and not just because I knew deep down—even though I did not want to admit it to myself—that my life hadn't been all that great.

I had wonderful children, yes. My relationship with my mother was better than it had ever been, yes. I did live with her, but the house was mine... *and the banks* a little voice reminded me. *But I'm making the payments.* It would be just mine someday.

I did not want to admit it, but I was truly sad because almost as deep down as the doubts within me hid, the truth lay. There was no going back. There was no changing the way things were. This was permanent and somehow, someday, I would have to find a way to make peace with leaving my entire world behind and go with him. And I knew it — even if I didn't want to know it.

I let go then, dropping to the ground with another sob.

It was no surprise that he caught me again, only this time, when the water whooshed around us, we ended up sitting across from each other at one of the small tables behind the bank in the outdoor covered break area they had built for us.

Fortunately, there was no one there because the bank was closed.

I looked at him and he looked at me, but no one spoke for what felt like minutes... or hours — it was impossible to tell. We were just sitting in absolute silence. I could feel his frustration and irritation flowing and ebbing over and through me as I sat there.

His thoughts were so wrapped up in his emotions that I couldn't separate them. They rushed through and around me like the strange water cloud we would disappear in — though there was no physical evidence visible — the feeling of disorientation was essentially the same. It left me feeling confused, frustrated and a bit irritated myself.

After another couple of minutes... or hours... I still couldn't tell, I put my hands down on the table in front of me. Hard. "All right. Stop it."

Immediately, the frenetic swoosh and swirl stopped. I breathed easier for a few seconds. Time started to move more like it should. Still, he said nothing. And, somehow, his thoughts were closed to me... or at least so much so that I couldn't get to them. I wanted to ask why — and before that curiosity got the better of me, I shook my head to clear it a bit more.

"Well, I'm gonna go now." I started to get up.

He put a hand on mine to stop me. "Please don't."

I could not tell if it was his power over me that made me stay, settle back down on the cool bench — or just the depth of emotion that was in those two words. But stay I did. I sat back down. I left my hand right where it was. I waited. I even tried to put a somewhat less angry and irritated expression on my face.

I had been certain only a few seconds before that time was moving at a normal pace again, but it felt like an eternity before he spoke again. It might have just been the amount of tension and maybe pain that I could see in his expression and feel in his touch, powers or no powers.

"There is more that you must know before you go back to your life." He stopped there, but I could see there was more, so I stayed quiet.

Waited.

I knew I didn't need to ask him what. He would tell me when he was ready. How I knew, I didn't ask myself. I did not want to take a chance on opening up the floodgates again. The reprieve from his emotions was too much a relief to risk bringing it on again.

He didn't speak. But I heard him—in my head, and then I was somewhere else... under the ocean again, looking out over the open water. I started to call the power I mostly had full control over now—to take me home.

But nothing happened. I turned to look at him.

"Please don't misunderstand me. It's not that I don't want to be here." I put up a hand when he started to move forward, relieved when he waited. "I have a family I cannot leave. You don't understand. You just cannot keep doing this to me."

He smiled then, but it was not a silly smile or even a happy one. It was more ironic and even a little angry as he spoke. "I think it is you who does not understand. I have an entire ocean to look after. My family is nearly endless, there are so many of them." He swept a hand beside and behind him as he spoke, trying to draw my attention to something, but I was not in the mood to play this game anymore. I refused to look.

He had moved closer as he had spoken, but he had not tried that heat... charm... thing of his yet, so my thoughts were still my own for the time being.

I was not at all sure how to take his words. Had he been thinking of his family when he'd abducted me? Had he been thinking of mine? Was he now? I wanted to ask, but the way he had spoken about his family, his responsibilities... had me worried.

If his reasons for abducting me had anything to do with his family, there was very little chance I would be able to change his mind or convince him my own family was more important.

If only I could figure out what it was he wanted from me. But, again, I was too afraid to ask him. None of what was going on made the slightest sense to me. So, we stood there... for so long that I completely lost track of time.

Then he stepped forward, moving so quickly I merely saw a blur of movement. He reached up and placed a hand on my cheek, his fingers at my temple, his thumb brushing my cheekbone.

There was a strange feeling, across my cheek, almost like water pouring across my face, and then my vision clouded over... only to be replaced by a horrific scene that took my breath away.

I was back under the ocean, looking down at what

I somehow knew was the same palace where he would have made me his Queen. Though, the palace I was looking at was nearly destroyed—and not gold, but a soft white like some sort of crystal. Several of the towering spires were completely missing. Every other tower was either blown open or blown apart.

And then there was the city below... it was in even worse shape. There was no smoke, but fires burned somehow. They burned the city to ash that floated up to form a dirty cloud around and over what little remained.

As I watched the scene unfold before me, mermaids and mermen swam free of the city. Some of them escaped. Some of them did not. They were mowed down by strange projectiles that were somehow familiar... but also not.

More of the city crumbled every second, and it was easy to see that there were far less of the people escaping than those that had been killed or were dying tragically... painfully... this very moment.

I could hear screams, so many... They were overlapping to create a strange wave of sound that flowed out and up from the remains of the city. It flowed into me and was somehow amplified... by what, I had no idea, but the pain was nearly unbearable.

The agony in my chest, the pain that made it impossible to breathe, was obviously not my own, though it was difficult to tell. The strength of it was overwhelming. I wanted to move forward, to do something, to stop the massacre.

But I knew... somehow... that I could not. I couldn't move. I would be seen. Without my full abilities, I would only be killed as well. And that would help no one. The thoughts were not entirely my own, but they were there, in my head, contributing to the pain I felt.

The city continued to burn. The screams kept sounding. The projectiles continued their assault. And I watched as far too many bodies joined the debris that was floating aimlessly and covering more and more of the city every second.

My people... The thought was like a mortal scream, wrenched painfully from my helpless body as I strained against whatever it was that was holding me back. There was tremendous resistance. No matter how much I struggled, I could not get free.

I was trapped, and not only in the spot where I was hidden, but in the agonizing thought that I was beginning to realize must be a memory. Had the man in front of me truly experienced this?

I wanted to beg him to stop, to release me, to ease the suffering, but there was also a part of me, something given to me by him no doubt, that took charge of my body, my emotions, my pain, and put it behind a barrier of sorts, somewhere that would protect the rest of me from its effects.

And then he did release me... from the memory.

It was painful.

Thankfully, he held tightly to me. It was the only thing that saved me from dropping to the ground. I found myself clinging tightly to him, leaning into the heat I had been mostly annoyed with thus far.

The memory had left me feeling drained, both emotionally and physically. Whatever he had done to me to share it with me had nearly been too much for my body.

Thank goodness I'm sitting down... was all I could think.

"I needed to show you that. I do apologize for the effect it had on you." Something in his tone told me he was not quite as sorry as he ought to be, but then, if what he had shown me was his own memory, then he had been through all of that himself with no one to shield or protect him from the effects it'd had on him.

When he spoke again, his voice was sad, nearly heartbroken. "I see now that I cannot stop you from going back to your life. Where we go from here, I do not know, but... I am sorry for how this was done to you."

"Thank you." The words tumbled out before I could stop them. I had expected something so much worse—and that relief was almost painful in its' arrival.

"That is not all." He went on—and I almost... almost cussed in my annoyance.

So close. I was so close. What else could there be? So, I

turned my attention back to him. Waited again.

"You may go back to your life as it is now, but there is also something you should know that will affect how your life goes forward."

"Other than all the freaky things you did to me, of course." I interrupted. I couldn't help myself.

He went on, no less calm than he had been before I jumped in with my comment. "Yes." But he stopped there.

I waited, but he didn't continue. Was he waiting for me to interrupt again? Was he trying to gather up the nerve? Just how bad was this whatever he had to tell me?

He closed his eyes then, took a deep breath, squared his shoulders. And, when he opened his eyes, there was definitely something like pain in them, a deep pain that nearly made me flinch with the intensity of it. It made me want to ask, but at the same time it made me terrified to know. Before I could stop him though, he started speaking again.

"As with the abilities, there is no way to sever this connection. Our world does not work the way yours does. This is something that is forever. I can do nothing about that. Your abilities can be controlled and you will be able to exist among the humans, but you will no longer age the same. At some point they will notice and you will need to take steps. I do not know enough about the way your world works, but I do know that humans tend to fear that which they do not understand. This will take some ingenuity on your part."

I let out the breath I hadn't even known I was holding. That was what was so bad. I could find a way to handle that.

"That is not all." I sucked in a breath. Waited again.

"You will not be able to form any sort of lasting connection with a human man." He stopped again.

I looked at him. Surely he was joking... *No. He doesn't joke.* His expression told me as much. It was perfectly serious. A mask of stone. I nearly laughed out loud. Was this way of telling me I would never get over him? Was this ego or just some attitude that came with being Sea King?

"It is not that." He might be blocking his thoughts from me, but clearly he had been listening in on mine. "You are unable to form any sort of lasting connection with a human male because we are bound."

"Yeah, that doesn't sound any different than what I was already thinking." I laughed this time. The nerve of him.

He closed his eyes, then just sat there. I started to ask what he was doing, but he stopped, looked right at me and spoke slowly—almost as if to a small child.

"You would say married."

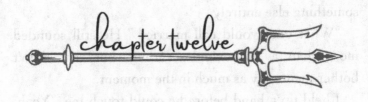

chapter twelve

I STUMBLED BACKWARDS OVER THE bench and stepped back quickly, certain that I could not have heard him correctly.

"We're what!"

He stood slowly, much more calm than I, and stepped around the table, slowly reaching out to me as he did. When I moved even further away, he stopped advancing—and then, when he answered me, he spoke very slowly, as if to a child.

"We are bound. Joined. Mated." He emphasized each word. And what was worse, he put some very intense images in his mind—his, not mine, but still...

when he said each one, images that might have overwhelmed me with desire just ten minutes ago. However, between his obvious condescension and the shock that had taken hold of my entire body, there was zero chance of any desire creeping in to overwhelm me in any way.

I had thought he was being egotistical, but this was something else entirely.

"What you would call married." He still sounded more than a little condescending, but that didn't bother me nearly as much in the moment.

I held up a hand before he could touch me. "Yeah. I got that before. What I want to know is how... and when? You couldn't just do this without my agreeing to it." As soon as the words were out of my mouth, I realized there absolutely was a way he could have done it without my agreeing. I had no memories of a ceremony binding us together. But then, I had very little memory of the time I'd spent underwater with him. I had no idea what a wedding to the Sea King actually involved. And since he had basically erased everything about me that made me *m e* for several hours of that day, I could've agreed to anything and not remember it.

He must have been listening in on my thoughts again because—though he didn't answer out loud, there were hazy, foggy memories swirling in my head. There was no sense to them. They were just a jumble of fog and confusion. This must be what I was wondering about, but either he was still trying to hide something from me or my own emotional state was messing with them because they just continued to swirl in a confused, jumbled mess.

I held up a hand. "And what exactly does that mean in human terms Is it just as binding as...?" I was afraid to finish the question. Deep down, I was sure I already knew the answer, but I needed to hear him say it. Out loud.

"I would like to say yes, but to be perfectly honest, no. Our way is quite different from what you humans think of as marriage." He paused there for just a moment before going on, and his tone actually became more serious... if that was possible. "Being bound is not at all the same for my people as marriage is for humans."

I started to open my mouth, mostly to spit another ugly comment at him... The man had not only changed everything about me, but he had somehow contrived to marry me, to bind me to him in some weird, fishy way. The fury seething within me was even more overwhelming than the desire from earlier had been, but something stopped me... gave me pause, made me really think.

It wasn't what he had said, but how he had said it —almost as if the way we humans viewed marriage had hurt him somehow.

So, instead I took a deep breath, let it out slowly, and then forced myself to speak softly. "What do you mean exactly, that it's not at all the same for my people as yours?"

He did step forward then, taking my hand in his before answering. "Darling, you must come to the realization at some point that you are no longer human." As he said it, he rubbed a thumb over my hand, softening his words impact a tiny bit. "You are part of my people now... in more ways than one."

I took a step back again—and when my legs bumped against the bed, I dropped down onto the soft surface, the uneven blankets and clothing still tangled underneath me only getting the tiniest bit of notice as I brought my other hand up to run it over my face before resting my forehead in my slightly curved palm.

"Boy. Every time. I tell you, every time I think I might finally start to get a hold on some part of this craziness, you hit me with something new—and I just... I just... I don't even know anymore." The emotions swamping me now were just too big, too numerous, too confused and jumbled and consuming.

He didn't let go of my hand, but he did crouch down on one knee in front of me.

"I know it must seem as though I am, but I promise you, I am not trying to make this more difficult for you."

I looked up then, gently placing the hand that had been on my forehead, on his cheek. "I know. It's just a lot to deal with... for anyone. But, especially for a

Mother of two from nowhere, more than slightly overweight, not exactly what you'd call flush, and just doing the best she can for her family."

He started to speak, but I moved my hand, placed a finger over his lips. "I know. You're going to argue with something I said about myself. I don't see myself very clearly."

He was nodding his head, but I went on without letting him speak up. "The thing is this. I've lived an unremarkable life. I'm not the only woman in the world with a deadbeat ex. I'm not the only single mom around. I'm not the only woman who had to move back in with her mother after her ex left her high and dry." I stopped for a moment, took a breath. Then went on.

"None of that makes me unique or fantastic or remarkable or even exciting. And I've mostly spent my life ok with all of that. I mean, if you'd shown up in my early twenties, when I was dreaming of going off to some exotic destination or alien world because absolutely everything in my life was just boring and I wanted to be anywhere else but where I was... well, I wouldn't have my kids, so that wouldn't have worked either."

He looked like he wanted to say something again, but I waved my hand to stop him and then kept going.

"I know. Just give me a minute to get this out. Please."

He nodded. I continued.

"In my teens and early twenties I wanted to be anywhere but where I was. I felt stuck. Bored. Trapped even. Then I met the children's father, and my life was interesting for a time. But other than the normal, everyday craziness that goes along with raising kids, there is nothing remarkable about my life —and there's just only so much I can deal with at a time."

He stood then, sat beside me and pulled me into his arms gently. No imagery rushed through me to stir up hormones. No power pulled me to him or made me want him. He was, in that moment at least, giving me exactly what I needed in the midst of being so very overwhelmed. He was simply holding me, letting me lean on his strength, giving me peace and quiet and comfort.

I lost track of time again while we sat there, curled together in the least romantic situation we'd been in since this whole crazy situation had started. I took advantage of the opportunity to just breathe —and to sit quietly, not worrying or thinking really... about anything... for a few precious moments.

How much time passed I would never be able to tell you, but when my breathing had completely returned to normal, the images rushing around in my head had finally slowed and stopped... which meant my head no longer felt as if it just might explode, I opened my eyes and looked around —and it took several seconds for me to register where we were.

His hotel room, of course.

How we'd gotten there I didn't have to ask. I knew exactly how he had whooshed me here. And the why was pretty obvious too. If he couldn't get me back under the ocean, he'd always bring me back here where he could have his way with me. And when that thought brought anger rushing back in to my mostly calm mind, I clamped down on it.

It wasn't at all what I had thought. He might have done it all under false pretenses... tricked me and taken away my memories of my life here, but he had not taken advantage of me in that way.

It wasn't much, but it was something.

He had bound us in whatever way his people had before taking me to bed. In fact, if the few memories I had of my time underwater were correct, he had missed out on his wedding night. I had no idea what ceremony I'd been preparing for when I'd begun to remember, but it would have to have been something that took place after the wedding—and I had spent that night in my own bed in my own house... far away from him.

Hmm... no wonder he was annoyed and crotchety when he came back for me. I couldn't help but laugh a little inside to think that he had been dealing with a very different sort of frustration than I had originally thought when he'd shown up there.

Before I could get too caught up in the humor of his predicament, I stopped to think back over the discussion/ argument we'd been having. When exactly had he brought us back here? How had I not noticed the swirling water around us and the instant change of scenery?

I didn't get a chance to wonder long. The sudden lack of warmth made me aware that he'd let go and sat back. He hadn't gotten up from the bed, but he had moved just far enough away that I could not feel the heat of his body... even the supernatural heat that he'd used to pull me closer so many times.

Are you quite finished?

His voice inside my head was more than a little annoyed—and it made me want to laugh all over again.

"Come on, you have to admit it is pretty funny."

He didn't acknowledge my words at all, just sat there looking at me.

"Can you at least admit it's good to find something funny about this whole, unfair, ridiculous situation?"

His lips twitched, but he still said nothing.

I scooted around on the bed until I was facing him, tucking one leg up in front of me as I moved. "Please at least admit that this is not an ideal situation?"

To that he, at last, nodded.

"To be perfectly fair, I think I've handled it much better than a lot of human women in my position would." He started to speak, but I held up a hand. "I know. I know. I'm no longer human." When he nodded again, I went on. "But I was. And I still think like one. I'm still going to behave like one. Everything I know is from the world of humans. Everything I feel. Everything I want. Everything I love or hate. How I forgive or not. You've got to understand that at least a little."

"It is not how it was supposed to be." He looked very unhappy when he said it, though he offered no further explanation... either in his thoughts or with his words.

"How was it..." But I didn't need to finish. I suddenly knew exactly what he meant. This was why he had taken my memories of my family, of my children, of my life here on Earth. I was only supposed to know his ways, the ways of the ocean, the ways of a Sea Queen—obedient, silent, bendable.

I expected anger to rise up within me, swamp me again, but all I could seem to muster was a swell of pity.

This was his way of finding a Queen, someone to spend countless years with him ruling over the oceans? He'd already told me I would no longer age like a human. He'd had parents. He'd grown up, so clearly there was some aging process his people went through, but it could be ten times as long as any human being. It could be a hundred times as long. I had no way of knowing. He would be stuck with a wife for hundreds or maybe even thousands of years who was only with him because he'd made her think she wanted to be. What could possibly be appealing about that?

He's clearly studied the human world. I know we're not always the best example, but is there literally nothing he's learned from watching us when it comes to love? The answer was obvious in seeing what he had done with his one and only chance.

And suddenly, I was immeasurably grateful I had not met him when I was a young twenty-something thinking all I wanted was a fantastical fairy tale in a world other than the one I'd grown up in. He might actually have convinced me that it would be a good thing to just run off with him—with nothing other than this supernatural attraction between us... no romance, no love, no emotion of any kind other than anger and frustration. How long could that supernatural ability of his bind a woman to him? Wouldn't he eventually want her to want him without him having to use his power to make her?

How long until it would take more and more and more to pull her to him? And when he tired of making her come to him, how would they go on with nothing to tie them together anymore? And that would go on for hundreds or even thousands of years. The words came out without my even intending them to...

"That is probably the saddest thing I think I've ever heard."

He sat thee for maybe ten full seconds, just staring at me before moving so quickly, I knew it had to have been water assisted.

That is how I missed it. He can do it so fast, it's pretty much instantaneous.

I wanted to ask how he'd done it so fast. I wanted to ask why he'd not done it so fast before, but I was too distracted by the man pacing the length of the room, muttering under his breath.

Since it was the first time I'd seen him not one hundred percent in control of himself and his emotions and words, I was intrigued. I didn't interrupt him. I was careful to hold my thoughts close. I simply watched, fascinated as he paced and muttered—looking more human by the minute.

His muttering was unintelligible, and his thoughts were no help. They were rolling over me, but not—for once—overwhelming me. It was not the same as it had been before. They were a jumbled mess, but he wasn't putting them into my head. It was more that they were just there, likely because of our new level of connection. *Oh joy. I wonder how far this connection reaches? Am I going to hear him, feel him when he's thousands of miles away at the bottom of the ocean? Will I never be free of him?*

That thought should have made me angry again, but I was still a bit too entertained by the image of said Sea King as he paced and muttered like a irascible child.

It went on for several more minutes before I started to get a bit bored. I wondered if I could get away with leaving or if he would stop me. Before I could try, he was standing in front of me, calmer now, quiet, his expression otherwise undecipherable. His thoughts were still a bit too roiling to interpret as well, so I waited.

He said nothing.

"I'm guessing you don't want me to leave. Though I'm not sure what else we really have to say to each other..." I paused significantly before adding, "... right now."

"Is that truly what you think? That I am some misogynist who took you away from your family—who cares nothing for you other than as a body to physically please me, a vessel to carry my children and a shell to sit beside me quietly and rule, bored and unhappy for all the years we are together?"

It wasn't precisely the way I'd described it in my head... *But close enough to the truth I suppose.* I started to say this out loud, but one look at his face told me I would be wasting my breath.

"I would never treat you so thoughtlessly. You were chosen through a most arduous process, one which took years to complete. My most trusted advisors assured me that you are my match in every way and insist even now that we will be even more strongly bound than my own parents."

"And in this little scenario, am I myself or who you convinced me I was—before I managed to remember my children? Did they tell you that would happen or how I would react to all this when it did?"

When he said nothing, I saw the truth in his thoughts and pushed on before he could stop me again.

"Humans don't work that way. We're not all so easily manipulated and we don't take too kindly to being stolen from our lives. We like having a choice to make. We enjoy our free will and do not behave rationally when it is taken away." I started to turn away, but another thought came to me, one that was too good to let pass.

"And in your studying of humans and life above the sea, did you ever learn anything about bears, specifically mother bears?"

He nodded slowly—and I could see for myself the imagery that was now flashing through his mind's eye.

"You know how mother bears are about their cubs..." He nodded again, a little slower than before. *Good. He's beginning to understand then.*

"I see." was all he said.

I waited, fully aware that I didn't need to press the point, reassured that we were finally communicating a little better, relieved that I didn't have to keep fighting him. I could feel him letting go a little in his thoughts. There was so much more than shame there. He was finally beginning to understand what he had done, how he had violated—not only my privacy and free will, but so much more.

"Do not think I am going away permanently."

Those words took me by surprise. His thoughts...

"I know. Thank you. Do not think because you can read what I am thinking in the moment, that you know everything about my innermost thoughts and decisions." His words were intense, but still sad.

"I suppose you are correct. We have a lot to learn about each other. And while we do that, perhaps we can find a solution that will work to everyone's best interest."

I could read between the lines of what he was saying—and I could see that he knew I was doing precisely that. "Well, I'll say this. You're definitely good at being diplomatic."

He smiled just a little at my words. They weren't precisely a compliment—and he knew that, but he was choosing to be as positive as possible.

He took my hand again—and then we were standing beside my car in the bank parking lot.

"We will see each other again soon." With that, he bent and kissed my hand—and I couldn't say why, but the way he was handling things compelled me to compromise... to meet him halfway somehow.

"How about we try dinner?"

When he straightened, he was smiling again, not wolfishly, not childishly, not triumphantly—just a nice, warm smile of genuine appreciation.

"I would like that very much. Tomorrow evening?"

When he accepted and gave me only a day to prepare, I panicked. I started to tell him that I had not one thing I could wear on a date with a Sea King, but he beat me to it.

"I will have something sent to you." I remembered that closet he'd had full of clothing and realized he had definitely prepared for this sort of thing.

Maybe he did foresee a bit of how difficult I could be.

His smile told me I'd hit that nail on the head as well.

"That sounds perfect. Thank you."

And then he was gone, disappearing in a swoosh of water again—and I stood there for several seconds before turning and getting into my car.

chapter thirteen

FRIDAY MORNING DAWNED CLEAR, bright and beautiful. The bank was closed on Fridays, so I had nowhere to go and nothing to do except think about my upcoming evening plans. The night before —not long after I'd gotten home—a large box had been delivered to the house... not at all what I had been expecting.

Of course, what I had expected was a whoosh of water and a beautiful outfit laid out on my bed like a royal command on Friday afternoon sometime.

This was not that at all. There were actually three different outfits for me to choose from, along with the clothes I had left in his hotel room—cleaned, pressed, and neatly folded at the bottom of the box. When I pulled them out, my mother made a small noise in her throat, but said nothing.

I had already told her what happened—pretty much all of it. Not every single detail, but enough for her to know what was going on and where we were at the moment. But I supposed it was entirely a different thing to hear the story—and to see the evidence right in front of you, folded neatly in a box.

Dylan had lost interest the moment he'd realized it was clothes for me and, fortunately, Cassie was busy dancing around the room with the dress she wanted me to pick, pretending to be a fairy princess—which was what she insisted I would look like if I wore it on my date.

A date that everyone seemed to have very different reactions to. I was apprehensive—no surprise there. Dylan could not have cared less if he tried. He had just shrugged and said "Whatever." when I'd mentioned it. Cassie was over the moon, asking all sorts of questions for which I did not have answers.

I imagine I could have reached out to his mind and found some or all of them, but I was half afraid he would show up early if I did... that, or misconstrue it in some way that would give him confidence he really didn't need. Mom was in the same ballpark as me, but for completely different reasons—obviously.

I had offered the olive branch because I could see

there was no making the mysterious Sea King go away and I was getting sick of fighting him on everything. Now, with time to think it over, I was beginning to feel ill over it. I had no idea what to expect and the clothes he had sent over did not make me feel any better.

It hadn't taken long for Cassie to bug me into trying them all on, ending with her favorite, of course. "Saving the best for last..." she'd said. And here I stood, in front of the only mirror in the house that almost gave me a full length look at myself.

They all had the look of designer clothing, but there was not a single designer label in any of the pieces. In fact, there was not a label anywhere on any of them. Nothing that mentioned size or care or anything of the sort. I couldn't help wondering if these items were things that might have been made for me as Queen—handmade by someone in his undersea palace. The fabrics prompted me to believe that was the most likely answer.

They were like nothing I had ever felt before... not that I'd actually felt the fabric you would find with a designer label. Added to that was the way they all conformed to the shape of my body, like they were meant to be worn underwater—where you wouldn't want things floating up and away from you. And, even though everything was fitted in ways that made me uncomfortable, not one item made unwelcome emphasis of the extra pounds I'd hated for years.

Rather, they took advantage of those curves in ways I wished designers would actually choose to feature.

I stood in front of the mirror and looked at myself, trying desperately to see whatever it was that he saw when he looked at me. Yes, the dress made me look curvy in all the right places and made every extra pound in a wrong place look almost nonexistent, but he had seen me in my ragged jeans and a baggy tee. He had also seen me naked—and he had looked at me with a hunger I had never seen on my ex-husband's face or the couple of guys I had been with before him... or the three dates I'd had since the divorce.

Was it just the supernatural pull? Did it affect him the same way it affected me? Could it maybe be affecting him more just because he was male? Sea King or not—he was still a man, wasn't he? Could that be all there was to it?

It has to be. I told myself.

Years before I was even married, I had figured out that the instant attraction in romance novels and the depth of feelings, lust, and the attraction those characters felt was all trumped up to make readers buy more books. It was pure fiction. Written for women so they could at least pretend it was real. No one in reality truly felt that way.

Right?

No. I told myself to stop fantasizing. I was doing this because he was not going away and we had to figure out some way to fix this. That was all. There was no way he was going to take me away from my family, my life I had fought so hard for, take away my freedom, my memories, the very essence of who I was.

We would simply have to figure out some way to fix it all. Fighting hadn't done that, so we were going to try another way. If he could be diplomatic, then so could I.

Looking back at my reflection, I asked myself the real question running around in my thoughts. Would it be more diplomatic to go with the sexy dress he'd sent? Part of me didn't care if it was or not. The way the material swished and swirled around my legs and the way it made my curves look positively fantastic was enough of a reason for me to never want to take it off.

"WOW! Mommy, I love that!" I hadn't even heard Cassie come in behind me, but with her exclamation came arms thrown around my waist in a tight hug. "I told you. Didn't I tell you it would be perfect? That it would make you look like a fairy princess!"

How about a Queen, love?

I didn't say it out loud. She didn't seem to understand just how real and frightening all of this was and I saw no reason to worry her with it... at least not until I had to, anyway.

"Are you gonna wear this one, Mom? Please say you are. Please?" She was bouncing up and down in her excitement, pulling at me in the process.

I laughingly untangled her arms from around my

waist and then leaned down toward her, hugging her tightly to me for a long moment before letting go again.

"I think you're right, sweetie. It does look the best on me. I don't know about making me look like a fairy princess, but I think I will wear it tonight."

"YAY!" She actually jumped when she yelled the word. And then she was gone to tell her grandmother and brother that she had convinced me to wear the dress she liked best.

Meanwhile, I sat down at the small desk in my room, pulled open the tiny makeup bag I only used for really, really special occasions—like job interviews or singing a solo at church. There wasn't much to work with—and I knew there was nothing I could do to have my makeup measure up to this dress. I didn't even want to start thinking about what I would do with my hair.

I felt more than saw or heard the change in the room behind me. Turning in my chair, my jaw dropped when I saw the three women standing behind me. They had appeared behind me with no noticeable whoosh of water, so I suspected he had to be behind it. They were dressed in what almost looked like mermaid tails around their legs—although they did have legs—and they were each carrying a bag full of things.

Supplies to do makeup and hair I'll just bet.

I couldn't help thinking the sarcastic comment, and

somewhere from far off, like it was coming down a long tunnel came his voice.

"Seemed like the least I could do."

I wanted to be annoyed, to feel as if he had taken some liberty he was not somehow entitled to, but the truth was far more frightening. There was a warmth spreading across my chest—gratefulness and something else I didn't want to deal with at the moment. It was something that no other men I had ever known would have thought of. He was taking care of me in such a simplistic way, I couldn't be annoyed or angry... no matter how much I might want to be.

Thank you.

I sent the message back to him, trying to keep it simple, but the phantom caress he sent back in return was not at all simple—and, something in my expression or body language must have told the three ladies, who had been busily winding curlers through my hair, because they erupted into fits of giggles. Although they said nothing, they blushed and smiled and continued to giggle while they kept working.

Since I had absolutely no idea what I could say, I remained quiet and let them do their work.

At some point, one of them—I had no idea of any names and I was inexplicably hesitant to ask—requested I close my eyes. I guessed so she could put makeup on them. However, after that I sort of lost track of time. It was easy to admit that it felt great to be pampered and primped like a princess. I just hoped whatever they were doing to my hair and makeup worked for land... and didn't freak out any of our human dining companions.

What they were doing, I had no idea, but I allowed myself to be painted and pulled, curled and brushed. At least it kept my mind off what the night ahead would bring.

"Your Majesty..." I was pulled out of my near doze by a small, hesitant voice right by my ear.

Opening my eyes, I was surprised to see that only one of the women remained. She had clearly been waiting for me to wake up.

How many times did she say my name, trying to get my attention?

I was a little embarrassed, but a glance at the clock told me it had only been about half an hour since I had sat down to do my makeup.

I looked back just in time to see her drop into a curtsy before disappearing in a whoosh of water. I shook my head at the oddness of it all. Here I had been dreading the night, worried about what I would wear... he'd taken care of that, worried about my hair and makeup... he'd taken care of that. I had nothing left to worry about.

Well, except the rest of the evening, anyway.

The thought did little to comfort the butterflies that had started up in my stomach. Desperate to distract myself, I stood and moved to the almost floor length mirror we had. To say that my reflection shocked me would have been an understatement. I looked like me... but I didn't.

There was no way to know what they had done to my hair, but it flowed down in curly waves that were so annoyingly perfect, I almost wanted to cry. Also, when I moved they did too—in a very different way than my hair normally did. They almost made it look like I was underwater again.

And the makeup was absolutely flawless. It looked like I was not wearing any makeup at all—and yet, they had perfectly highlighted both my eyes and my lips in a way that I had never been able to get the hang of... and probably never would.

Before I had time to do more than wonder if they had used some sort of underwater magic to achieve both effects, the sound of a hard, confident knock on the front door—so strong I could hear it all the way down the hall—sent my heart into my throat.

That has to be him. No one else I know would knock that way on a door. Plus, a human would just use the doorbell.

"I have never understand the human's dependency on such silly things. Why use a device that makes a funny sound when a strong fist is just as effective?"

I had no idea how to respond to him at the moment. I had to admit, he had a point—though I knew there was also an argument for doorbells that I'd heard... possibly used in the past. I simply could

181

not figure out what it was.

"There. See. I am correct." The smug tone in my head should have been funny. It should have been distracting too, but it was neither—and I was too busy trying not to panic to notice that Cassie had come into the room, presumably to tell me he was here.

"I know. I know. I heard." I fluttered my hands in a way that most adults would have picked up on as a sign that I was panicking. Fortunately, Cassie was oblivious... only interested in my makeup and hair— which she'd just noticed.

"Mommy, you look so beautiful. Can you make my hair do that?" I had a tiny moment to be thankful she hadn't witnessed the entrance or exit of the women he'd sent to make me look like this before panic crept in again. How would I explain to my young daughter that I hadn't done this to my hair, much less have any idea how to do it to hers.

Luckily, my mother chose that moment to arrive, shooing Cassie away as she came into the room. Looking me over, her lips pursed in a way that told me she was not at all happy about the way I looked— even though there was also a glint of appreciation in her expression. She said as much a moment later.

"Well, you certainly do look breathtaking—though I'm not at all sure I want to send you out with that man looking so beautiful."

I laughed a little and threw my arms around her. "Oh! I love you, Mom."

She hugged me back tightly for longer than she usually did before letting go and stepping back.

"I won't promise not to wait up, but please let me know if I should... you know... go on to bed." She blushed a little as she said it—and I felt a similar blush rise up over my cheeks.

Before I could say anything though, she went on. "Just don't go disappearing under the ocean again please."

I laughed again and pulled her in for another tight hug. I wanted to reassure her that I would not be staying with him all night, and that I would certainly not be going off under the ocean with him again, but I knew both were promises I could not make with any degree of certainty. If he got it into his head that I would not cooperate, I would not put it past him to try taking all of my memories and sneaking me off to his undersea kingdom again.

So, instead, I just hugged her a little tighter for a few more seconds, until she said, "Well, you'd better not keep him waiting, I guess." There was that southern hospitality rearing its head again. She couldn't be rude if she wanted to.

"I love you, Mom."

"Now, why does that sound like you're making fun of me, I wonder?" She tried to sound annoyed, but spoiled it with a laugh.

"I dunno. It must be your imagination." I said it breezily, like I had done so many times before, but there was something different about it this time. Before I could examine it too closely, she was ushering me out of the room, barely giving me time to grab the tiny clutch I'd laid on the bed with all I hoped I'd need for the evening.

Moving down the hall, I paused in Dylan's doorway. He was playing a video game... as usual. I leaned in a little, watched him for a few seconds. Marveled at how much he had changed over the last year. He wasn't my little boy anymore. Nowhere near.

"Hey bud, homework all done?"

He let out his breath in what I was learning to be a typical teenage style huff of annoyance.

"Yes, Mom."

"Ok. Well, I'm going on my date now."

"Yeah. Have fun." He didn't turn his head or take even one of his hands off the controller.

"Don't stay up too late."

A sigh this time. "I won't."

"Good. Well... good night, sweetie."

"Night."

I stood there for another second or two, shaking my head. Would I ever understand teenagers?

Cassie was there at the entrance to the hallway when I turned away from Dylan's door, bouncing up and down in place in her excitement. She didn't run to me, but waited for me to walk to her. The closer I got, the harder she bounced.

He must look like what she thinks a fairy prince looks

like. In my head, there was his unmistakable presence, smug again. *Stop that, won't you please?*

"No, I don't think I will. Your daughter likes me. I only need to get the other two on my side—and then perhaps you will see reason."

Not very likely.

This entire exchange took place while I walked across the room, Cassie beside me, bouncing with every step. Mother stood close enough to reach out and touch the Sea King, but held herself stiffly away from him at the same time. She didn't have her arms crossed over her chest, but her face said 'stay away' to anyone who cared to look.

He wasn't looking at her. He didn't even seem to notice my dress, my hair, or makeup. His eyes were locked with mine, looking at my face with such a deep intensity, I could feel the heat from across the room... all the way to my toes.

I wanted to be flattered. I wanted to be annoyed— he had gone to such lengths to send me such a sexy outfit—and the women to make my hair and makeup magical—and he wasn't paying a bit of attention to any of it. But I couldn't seem to hold on to anything beyond the warmth that was filling me up.

Cassie broke the spell. I took a deep breath, shaking my head at mother when she looked like she might rush over to me. What had just happened? What had he almost done? What had I almost done? One look at my happily bouncing daughter told me she hadn't noticed a thing. That gave me a small amount of comfort. If either of us had started building a wall of water around us, she would have noticed — and she would be all over me asking a million questions.

"Shall we go?" He spoke calmly, far more calm than I ever felt when he was around. Again, I felt like I should be annoyed, but I couldn't seem to muster even the smallest amount.

"I was hoping we might have a few minutes to talk before you go, get to know you a little better." This came from my mother — who was obviously hesitant to let me out the door when I was so obviously under the man's spell.

I was thankful for this. Not only could I use a few minutes to get myself under control. I wanted to know the answers to any questions she might ask him. I was also curious to see just how he would answer. He might know how much I had told my mother about him and the situation because of that bond we shared, but he would also know I had not told my children anything. How would he tap dance around her questions.

"That would be fine. What would you like to know?" He surprised me. His voice was warm and inviting, not at all hesitant. Anyone else would think he was a perfectly open book. I knew it wouldn't be that simple.

"Well, for starters, we don't even know your

name."

He leaned smoothly and effortlessly into a low, sweeping bow. "My apologies. Nicholas Thalass at your service."

Finally, I know his name.

It was certainly a relief. Finally I had something to call him.

Not that I actually need to know his name to call him.

Still, it would be good to know what to call him without the embarrassment of having to ask myself. Though I couldn't help but notice he specifically did not mention a title—and I was surprised to hear a last name. Did royalty usually have a last name? Didn't they usually go by some name that had more to do with their title or the family they were born into?

"Of course we do, but His Royal Majesty, King Nichola Mali Thalass Poseidon of the house of Okeanos sounded like a bit much for your daughter. You can always relay that to your mother at a later time if you wish."

No. Thanks I'm good. I think.

"As you wish."

I stared. Had he really just said "As you wish" to me? His smug grin was all the evidence I needed to know he had said those words—that way—on purpose, which meant he must have pulled the reference from my head at some point. How, I didn't want to know.

"I believe you know how by now."

Yeah, I guess I do, but do you have to do that? You're talking in my head. No one else can hear you. Can't you just say what you mean?

"So, you'd prefer me to announce to your family that I am madly in love with you, that I would like to take you to the bottom of the ocean, where you will be my Queen." It wasn't asked like a question—more like a statement of what he would do if I didn't stop him.

Actually, I'd really rather you didn't do all of that right this second. They barely know you. Lots of weird stuff has been going on—stuff I still have no way of explaining. Let's just give them some time to get to know you while I figure out what I'm going to do, please.

"As you wish."

The already wolfish grin deepened a little.

Beside me, my mother gritted her teeth so hard, I heard them snap together. So, she'd noticed our internal exchange. I was certain I would have to explain later what we'd been discussing. Just not right this second.

Cassie had started bouncing again at the way he said his last name, Tail-uh. I was certain this was some sort of ancient word for ocean or sea, but all Cassie heard was Tail—and since she was still obsessed with the mermaid tail I'd yet to be able to explain, hearing his name was enough excitement to

188

get her going all over again. She started to open her mouth, but mom stopped her from spouting anything about mermaid tails, by asking another question.

"So, what's the plan for this evening?" I had to admit, I was curious about the very same thing.

To which he replied, with a perfectly straight face, "Well, I thought we'd start with a little dinner, after which we'll run away together. See you in about a month. That is the standard honeymoon length, isn't it?"

My mother didn't miss a beat. "But you haven't packed. I guess you'll be shopping as you go, then?"

Cassie took my hand. Squeezed it tight. Clearly, she thought they were being serious.

"Guys..." I said, trying to use my best 'mom' voice. To Cassie, I said, "Sweetheart, they're only kidding." Then, back into 'mom' voice, I turned back to them. "Tell her you're only kidding."

My mother scooped her up and snuggled her close before answering. "Of course we're kidding. Aren't we?" She turned to the oh, so arrogant Sea King then with a look that I'd seen many times in my life. It was a look that said he had better not do anything to hurt her precious grandchild or he would regret it to the end of his days.

"Of course, we are kidding. I would not take your mother away from you for a whole month."

I said nothing in the moment, barely allowed myself to even think anything. It was entirely possible he was lying. I wouldn't know. But I realized, in that moment, I might have just done the very best thing I could have done, inviting him to dinner... giving him a chance to come here and really meet my family, see how much they loved me, needed me, how devastated they would be without me.

"Well, ok." I could see that Cassie was not going to be pacified by a stranger's word—especially after he'd made such a joke in the first place.

I stepped in front of my mother, looking my daughter in the eye, while speaking in my most reassuring tone. "Cassie, do you think I would run off and leave you?"

She threw her arms around me, pulling me closer to my mother. "No, Mommy. I don't."

"All right then." I turned to look behind me, pulling them with me as I did. "We won't be making any more jokes like that, then, will we?"

With a perfectly straight face again, he answered solemnly. "No, of course not. I am sorry to have upset you, Cassie dear. It was not at all my intention."

And, in the obliviousness and innocence of a child, she took him at his word. "Ok." And that was it. She slid out of her grandmother's arms and wrapped her arms around my legs again, squeezing a little before letting go. "Have fun tonight, Mommy."

Then, with a cautious look at Nicholas, she skipped off in the direction of her room. Ok, so maybe she hadn't completely taken him at his word.

That's my girl.

I watched her skip down the hall, turn and wave at me one more time before disappearing into her room. Before I could turn back to face Nicholas, my mother spoke.

"All jokes aside, there will be no running off, or taking her away." I opened my mouth and Nicholas looked like he wanted to say something as well, but she rushed on. "Spend the night together. Even the whole night. I won't judge, but she had better be back here first thing in the morning. I mean it." She had moved closer to Nicholas as she talked, advancing with each word and speaking in the most serious tone I'd ever heard her use.

It was impressive to behold... at least to me.

To Nicholas it was impossible to tell—until he answered her.

"I am certain if I tried to take her away, she would simply come back on her own. As she has before."

"Right." Mother looked a whole lot more confident than I felt, but I didn't take time to argue or even interject.

In fact, before I could think to say anything, Nicholas turned to me again, held out his hand. "Ready to go, my love?"

I felt more than heard the tiny gasp from my mother at his choice of words. He might be King of the seas, but I really needed to explain the importance of not 'poking the bear' where my mother was concerned. However, at the moment, I could only sigh and nod.

"I'll be back, mother. Dawn at the latest."

And then we were disappearing in that all-too-familiar whoosh of water.

chapter fourteen

WHEN WE ARRIVED IN HIS HOTEL room, I first wanted to laugh, but when I turned to him, and saw that he already had that look in his eyes, laughing was suddenly the furthest thing from my mind.

I had a moment, but only a moment to think what a waste it was that I would not get to show off this dress and how fabulous I actually looked in it to the other diners at the restaurant. But then he was pulling me toward the bed—and he must have done the water too fast for me to see because the dress was laying over a chair I could see on the other side of the bed.

And then we were falling onto the bed and into each other.

Thankfully, he didn't starve me. We did have dinner, just not in a restaurant. It arrived in his room, delivered by room service and set up at the table by the balcony doors.

It was the first time I had really paid a lot of attention to his room. What I had originally thought was a door to the hall, was actually a door to the rest of what turned out to be a suite... not just a room. The bedroom we were in was one of three and likely the largest. Once the waiter had gone, I'd come out, dressed in a nightgown I had found in the enormous closet. Someone had set up dinner on a smallish table next to a large set of doors leading out to a larger balcony. The doors were open, letting in the cool evening air and the sounds and lights of the city below.

It was all ridiculously magical, romantic, the perfect sort of date for two people in such an odd situation just trying to figure out what to do about it —and yet, the first words out of my mouth had nothing to do with any of that.

"You know, this is the digital age..."

He only smiled. Which meant either that he had no idea what I meant or he was humoring my crazy comment that was so very out of place.

As the heat of embarrassment climbed my neck, I moved out onto the balcony, hoping the cool air would at least help to cool the burning in my cheeks and neck.

Only a moment later, his arms came around my waist—and I could feel his breath at my ear as he whispered, "I do love how you worry for me."

Of course he knew what had been going through my mind—the long list of thoughts that had provoked such an out-of-place comment. How he popped in and out of his hotel room constantly, no cameras in the hotel lobby capturing his travel to and from. And then he ordered room service.

He didn't speak this time, simply shared his thoughts with me while his lips did very interesting things to my neck.

"As far as anyone in this hotel knows, I checked in and have not left the room since."

He slowly moved up my neck, nibbling at my ear and cheek with glorious attention. And all the while, his hands worked their magic, distracting me from whatever it was I had been thinking.

"You were thinking you do not want anything to happen to me. You are very concerned for my safety. You would not want my true identity being discovered by your

scientists. You worry they will take me away and turn me into a lab rat."

He turned me in his arms before going on.

"You have nothing to worry about, my love. I will not be discovered."

And then we both pretty much stopped thinking coherently.

At least we made it back to the bed somehow... was my first thought later—while my heart rate slowed to a more normal rhythm. Then, when my body made me aware of other needs...

You know, our food is probably cold by now.

There was a definite laugh in his response.

"Why do you think I ordered dishes that did not need to stay warm?"

You thought of everything, didn't you?

Somehow, that knowledge gave me a feel of daring I was not expecting. I rolled and shifted until I was straddling him, more than a little gratified at the look of astonishment. I had taken him by surprise. Him.

I guess we can eat later then.

We never did talk about any of the things I'd wanted to talk about with him on the date. We did eventually get to dinner—which was, surprisingly, just as delicious as when it had been brought up to the room. Some of it even ended up back in the bed with us later.

And, when some internal clock told me that dawn was imminent, I reluctantly climbed out of bed and went to find clothes to change into—clothes that would not tell my children what I had been doing all night.

Either he was completely worn out—and not roused by my thoughts or the noises I could not help making as I dressed and made my way to the bathroom, where I was surprised to find all of the things I had in my own bathroom—the hand soap I used, lotions, even the brush I used. The color was slightly different, but it was the exact same brand. It could have been a coincidence, but I was certain it was not.

He'd stocked the closet for me. Clearly, he'd done the same in here. Some part of me wanted to be angry for some reason. I really wasn't sure why. It wasn't like it was any worse an invasion of privacy than everything else he'd done. He had likely just plucked the memories out of my head and sought out duplicates.

Or... whoever put all this together for him did it.

I wondered about that. Would he have a way to put his thoughts into the heads of his subjects. The women he had sent to help me with hair and makeup. Had he just sent them a psychic message—or had he teleported himself underwater to relay the message himself?

Still too many questions.

A moment later, when I walked out of the bathroom and saw him lying there, watching me with that intense gaze of his, I wondered how long he had been listening in to my thoughts.

"Not long."

Hmm was my only response.

"Do you have to go?

"Yes. I promised my mother I would be home before dawn and it's nearly dawn now." I could see that was not the answer he wanted—and in my mind I saw what he planned to do next.

Taking a step back from where I had been—and putting a hand out in front of me gave me the perfect position when he appeared in that swirling tube of water just inches from me, still naked, still rumpled from the night we had spent together.

"I'm going." Then, before he could say anything else, "Surely, you don't want to break a promise you made to my family the first time you've properly met them. You wouldn't want to make me go back on my own word to my mother." When he said nothing, thought nothing, I took another step back and concentrated, brought the water that would take me home. It was getting easier every time I did it. That was good news at least.

The water had no more than begun to dissipate around me than I felt him beside me.

I looked up at the sky, torn between fright and curiosity. Had he appeared in the same state I'd left him or had he managed to show me up once again — and appear and dress simultaneously?

"We have nothing to be ashamed of. I came for you. I will bring you home."

His words sort of gave me my answer, but I sneaked a quick peak just in case... letting out a breath of relief when I saw, not only had he dressed, but he was wearing something different than he had been when he picked me up the evening before.

When I reached for the doorbell, he held out a small bag to me.

It was not the bag I had packed for our date, but it was a similar size and his self-satisfied smirk told me he had used his abilities again — and moved everything from one bag to another... all while dressing and transporting himself to me.

"Show off."

He said nothing, just stood there with that royal

smirk that—so help me—I was beginning to find much less annoying. It was becoming almost cute. And, that part was annoying.

Pulling my keys out of the small bag, I turned back toward the door and jabbed the key in the lock, forcing myself to take a breath and calm down before actually unlocking the door. It would not be a good idea to wake everyone up with my coming into the house so early. He might insist we had nothing to be ashamed of, but since I had not explained to my children that we were actually married—mostly because I had no idea how to—I really didn't want this to be the catalyst for that conversation.

I unlocked the door, started to open it, and then stopped. Was he planning to come in with me? That would be just as difficult to explain as it would be to tell them why I was only just now coming home.

"I had no intention of coming in. I only wanted the opportunity to deliver you to your door."

No surprise he'd been listening to my thoughts. Before I could say anything though, he turned me around and captured my mouth with his.

"And to do this one more time before I let you go, of course."

As usual, I completely and totally lost track of time while he kissed me. It spun out and stretched into a millennia while his lips did clever things to mine and his hands roamed over my back, slipping down to my rear after a time and pulling me even closer against him while those lips travelled down to nibble at my ear.

And then, rather abruptly, he stopped, stepped back. I struggled to regain my balance... in more ways than one. Fortunately, he still had a loose hold on me, so I didn't fall over. I just probably looked a little silly. As far as regaining any balance in the tumult of hormones, that might take longer.

However, one look at his face told me why he had abruptly stopped kissing me and moved away. Someone had opened the door behind me. I could only hope it was my mother. Not one of the kids.

The decidedly annoyed "hmm" coming from behind me answered that question—and dumped a metaphorical bucket of cold water over any lingering desire. Definitely my mother. And, despite his reassurance that we did not need to be ashamed of anything, I felt the heat born of embarrassment fill my face, my ears, my neck.

"The sun is up. That would be a bit past dawn if I'm not mistaken." Her voice was still annoyed, but I thought I could hear just the tiniest bit of humor somewhere in there too.

Maybe.

"We arrived before dawn." And he left it at that.

Mom said nothing, but she did cock an eyebrow at him. I looked down at the floor, the heat still holding control of most of my face.

Yeesh, Nicholas. I mean it's not like Mom can't

figure it out, but come... on... You could have been a little less... I dunno...

I stopped there though. There was no explaining — at least not by me... to him — how he could have explained better to my mother that he just had to have one more moment to remind me just how impossible it was becoming to resist him.

"I am King of the Seas. I have no need to explain myself to anyone."

His words were so unexpected, though they probably shouldn't have been, I very nearly laughed out loud. Here I had almost convinced myself he was getting just a bit less imperious.

"With you, my Queen, yes. Not with someone who questions my wanting to spend an extra moment with my wife before I must leave her... until she decides it is convenient to spend more time with me."

I almost... almost felt bad at his words — until I remembered just how we had gotten to where we were. Then, it was all I could do not to let the anger overwhelm me again.

Are your people's emotions always so much more difficult to control than ours — or is it just the added power boost to a human that makes it so? I knew there was more than a little bit of mean in my voice, but I was beyond caring in the moment. If he could go back and forth so unexpectedly, so could I!

"Please accept my apology, my love. I had no

intention of being imperious with your mother." He looked down at his feet before going on. *"I will do better."*

I wanted to believe him. I wanted to let it go and just get on with my day. I wanted not to have to deal with the fallout of all of this—with my mother, with him, with my children, who would have to be told about all of this eventually. I really wanted to just be out of this whole situation... to go back to my boring little life and just be normal again.

The strange sound that came from somewhere above me, coupled with the hard set of his mouth when I looked up at him told me he had been listening again to my thoughts. The strange noise must have been his teeth snapping together and he was now clenching those teeth together. Hard. Either it was to keep himself from saying something he might regret... *Not that it would matter, since he could just put the thought into my head...* or he was simply reacting to my thoughts. I was tempted for a moment to look, but I stopped myself.

I really didn't want to know.

Another sound of annoyance came from behind me. I had forgotten for a moment that my mother couldn't hear what we'd been saying. Would I ever get used to all of this internal speech?

Probably not.

Before I could say anything... or even think anything, he stepped back, leaned gracefully into a sweeping bow and said, "Until tonight."

Then he was gone—in a swoosh of water that elicited a gasp from my mother.

chapter fifteen

THIS WAS NOT THE FIRST TIME SHE'D witnessed his power, but I knew exactly what she must be feeling. I hadn't completely gotten used to it yet—and I could do it all on my own. I would probably have gasped too, if it hadn't been for all the million other things frustrating me and stressing me out about the whole situation.

At this point, a little watery disappearing act was nothing all that exciting. More annoying. Showy.

I took a deep breath before turning to face her. My annoyance had nothing whatsoever to do with her and everything to do with his royal splashiness and his determination that he would just continue to get his way.

"Until tonight indeed!"

I didn't realize I had spoken aloud until I heard my mother ask, "What was that, sweetheart?"

I took another breath and shook my head a little before answering. "Nothing important, Mom."

Finally, I turned to face her. She stood there, seemingly calm but for the expectant look on her face. It was fair. She had questions. I could almost feel them filling the air around her, the air between us, the air around me. I could only be certain that I would not have all the answers. Only the stupid Sea King had all the answers—and he had not stuck around to answer them.

No sooner had I thought it than I heard what sounded like a devious chuckle in my head.

Don't even think about coming back here right now. Questions or not, my children will be up any minute and I have no intention of trying to explain to them just what you are doing here so early.

He didn't appear—and he didn't chuckle again, but there was a feeling of enjoyment that was certainly not coming from me. And, like everything else about this ridiculous situation, there was absolutely nothing I could do about any of it.

Not one thing.

This time there was a different sort of feeling. A sort of triumph or—at the very least—excitement.

There might be nothing I can do about these abilities, about our stupid underwater marriage, about your ridiculous attachment, but there is certainly something I can do about your intentions. You know taking away my memories doesn't work. You also know that I can bring myself right back if you somehow manage to drag me underwater.

"That may be true, but you cannot run from this forever. One day there will no longer be anything to hold you on the land. What will your excuse be then?"

That one hurt. The pain wasn't just in my heart. It went all over, from the top of my head to the tips of my toes. I remembered him mentioning that I would no longer age like a human, but I had not put together just what that would mean for me... and for those I loved on land.

It wasn't just a question of losing them to old age. I would be forced to leave them at some point before that. People would notice if I stopped getting older... at least, older the way they would expect me to. And I'd seen enough television shows and movies to know what our government would do to me in that instance. And they probably wouldn't stop with me. They would want to know why I was aging differently from my family.

They would stick all of us in little white rooms and test us for who knew how long.

Well... not all of us.

I knew they wouldn't really be able to hold me, but would I be able to use my ability to get every other family member out? And where would they go once someone was looking for us? There would be no place on this earth I could hide them.

No place on this earth...

I turned toward the door before I remembered that my mother was still standing behind me, waiting for answers to the questions she had. So, I turned back. "Mom, I know you've got questions and you have to know I don't have all the answers. And I know the children will be up any second, but there is something I have to do right this minute and it cannot wait."

Her expression told me she knew exactly where I was going. I wanted to defend it, but I knew it would take far too long to explain—and I had the strangest feeling that if I didn't ask this question as soon as possible, something was going to happen to mess it all up. Make it impossible. Too late or maybe even something worse.

"I know. I know. I just got back. But..." I held up a hand before she could interrupt me. "I promise, I will explain everything the moment I get back."

She started to speak again, but again I held up a hand and stopped her. "I won't be more than an hour. Maybe less." And then I pulled the same trick he had only minutes ago... or maybe even just moments. I disappeared in a column of water.

His expression when I appeared—all on my own, with little to no warning, in his fancy hotel suite—was nearly priceless. When I started to speak, he stopped me.

"I know what you are going to say."

I didn't let that deter me one bit. "I know you do. So...?"

He did look perplexed at that. "So...? What?"

"What? You know what I was going to say. You had to know I was going to ask if it was possible. So... is it? Possible?" I added, when he still looked at me with confusion coloring his expression.

He stopped speaking at that point. *"You tell me you do not want to be forced into this situation. You are unhappy with me for what I have done to you. And now you expect me to what... do the same to your family, just so you do not have to leave them behind? Just how is that any different than what I have done to you?"*

I did speak. Somehow I felt I could get my point across better with actual words. "It's better because I won't be forcing them to do it. If you tell me it can be done, I can present them the opportunity. They can make the decision all on their own." I didn't add the 'ha', but I knew he heard it in my thoughts. He would have had to. It was right there at the very top of my mind. I didn't even care if it bothered him. If only he would tell me there was a chance I would not have to leave them behind.

"I do not know if it is possible. No one has ever done such a thing."

"So, all those stories about sirens falling in love with the men they were supposed to lure to their deaths—and instead, they take the men to live with them underwater..."

"They are stories." His thoughts gave me the distinct impression that he thought I must be very slow indeed to believe such nonsense.

"It is not nonsense. Every story has to have some truth to it. If people know about sirens, there must have been instances where someone saw one and lived to tell the tale."

Now he spoke aloud. "I am not denying that there is a possibility that humans have seen sirens or mermaids at one point or another. I am simply saying that there is not likely truth to the stories about a siren taking a human under the sea to live with her happily ever after—and someone witnessing it to *tell the tale* as you call it."

"And why not? If a human saw a siren take a human under the water—and then saw that human alive later, wouldn't that prove the story? Or maybe the person even came back some time later to tell the story themselves?"

Now he slipped back into thought. *"And why would he do that, pray tell? If he were brought underwater by a siren, he would not remember his life on land after the change required. And indeed, if he were living happily ever after with his siren, why would he even feel the need to set foot on land again?"*

"I am only saying it's a possibility." I spoke softly now, incensed that he was not more excited about the chance I was giving him. He would be getting his way, but I would, too. More frustrated than angry now, I crossed my arms over my chest as I prepared to leave.

"No." He started in thought, but went on aloud. "Please do not go. You are right. I am being unnecessarily dismissive of your idea. I never thought about what you propose. I do not know if it would be possible or not. It would take some study."

His words kept me from going, but they didn't really tell me if he was on board with the idea or not.

"I would like to be. I will have to speak to my advisors. To the historians. To my knowledge, such a thing had never been attempted. It may not be possible."

"But you will speak to them? You will find out if it is possible? Because if it is..." I didn't get to finish. He stopped me with a very impromptu hug.

"Yes, I will ask them. I do not know if you will like the answer, and I beg you to keep an open mind if the answer is not what you want to hear."

I was nodding before he stopped talking. "I will. I promise. Just the chance is enough to tell me you are trying to make this work. That makes me feel better about so many other things."

"And if the answer is what you want... And your family is not in favor of the solution?" His words were spoken slowly, cautiously, almost like he hated to even voice them.

I hadn't thought of that. Would they go along with this mad idea? Would they just think I was crazy? Would they... I stopped myself. There was no point in making myself crazy before I even knew whether there was a proposition to put to them or not.

He'd clearly been listening in again.

"I will go and find out then—whether there is something to this idea of yours or not."

Thank you. For the first time since showing up, I answered with my thoughts. It felt like a needed concession. He was going to give me what I needed. I could meet him halfway. This time.

"I do not know how long the search for this answer will take. I may be away for some time."

I could understand that. It would also give me the time I needed to figure out what I would do if the answer was no.

I would need to know how to deal with that possibility too.

He embraced me again, held me there for a very long moment before pulling me in for a shockingly gentle kiss, his arms never leaving my back. His lips never leaving mine. It felt like more than a simple, 'I'll see you soon' sort of kiss. I wondered at it, but didn't ask—even in my thoughts. And, after a few lingering seconds, he finally did break the kiss, stepped back. His hands moved to grip my upper arms tightly. He looked at me for another very long moment.

And then he let go and the water came, the whoosh and transfer taking a lot longer than any I had ever seen from him. Usually, he was just there one second and gone the next. This time, it was like he was taking his time. He looked at me the whole time—as the water built and twisted around him in a large column, his eyes looking into mine through the wall of water.

Then he was gone—and the room felt strangely empty. Cold. Lonely.

I stood there for another few seconds, attempting to rub some warmth into my arms before I called up my own water and whooshed my way back to the kitchen where my mother waited with her questions... some I still would not have any answers to. But I had promised to go back—and answer what I could.

I consoled myself by believing it didn't matter that I couldn't tell her exactly what I had come to ask him about. I would have those answers soon enough. I would tell her then.

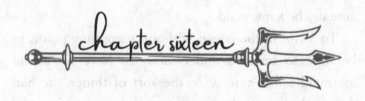

chapter sixteen

WHEN I RETURNED TO THE KITCHEN, I was not as surprised as I should have been to see my darling daughter sitting right next to her grandmother.

Her face was not the least bit surprised or frightened to see her mother suddenly appearing in the middle of the kitchen in a column of water. Granted, she'd seen it before... several times now, but the look of excitement on her face told me what her answer would be—if Nicholas came back and gave me the answer I really wanted.

Not that I really needed that for confirmation. My

sweet little girl, who had always been like a little fish in any body of water, and who had been so excited by my tail—wanting only to know if she could have one —had always joked that she was part mermaid. In fact, she had likely felt like she really was part mermaid, or had wished it were so. I was certain, at the very least, she would jump at the chance to actually be a mermaid.

To swim in the ocean without a stopping point, to be able to breathe underwater, to have an actual mermaid tail. These were the sort of things she had dreamed of since the first day I had jumped into the water with her at the local community pool.

She had worn floaties then, but it'd been no time at all before she was paddling around under her own power, no longer in need of a life preserver of any kind. She'd been nearly fearless, jumping into the pool before anyone else could even reach the edge. Then diving into the deep end. Then she had learned to swim like a mermaid, kicking both feet at once and shooting across the pool underwater with her powerful stroke and an impressive lung capacity.

She, at least, would welcome the opportunity. And she would want to stay with her mother, no matter what. So I didn't have to ask her what she would choose.

If his answer is the one I am hoping for...

I would have to wait to find out. We all would. And in the meantime, I would have a chance to feel out the rest of the family about what they would choose.

Dylan could go either way. He might want to join us on this unexpected adventure. Or, he might just rather stay on land... where he could play video games —and move in with his father, who would hopefully jump at the chance to spend more time with his son.

Mom was the real wild card. There was very little —since she had retired at least—other than us, to hold her on land. But would she want to make such a change? Would she want to give up the life we had so carefully built, let go of her computer and her television, her car and her normal life... the only life she had ever known?

It would be just as frightening for her as the whole thing was for me. And I didn't really look forward to even broaching the subject. The pain of having to choose—of knowing that one day soon, I would lose them all. Because, whether I chose to join him under the ocean now... or later, I would lose them when it became obvious that I was no longer aging as any other human.

I would not take the chance on exposing them to government scrutiny or experimentation. They would not become guinea pigs in some sick, twisted search for immortality... especially since I would be the one who they would need to experiment on. And, I knew somehow that Nicholas would never let that happen. He would, I was fairly certain, go to some pretty extreme lengths to keep me out of the government's hands.

He wouldn't exactly want his people exposed either.

That was a sobering thought. All this time, I had been worried about what would happen to me if I were discovered. I had never thought about what would happen with the rest of the people he protected.

Yes, he had command of the oceans, but did that mean he could stop every human who had ever dreamt of finding a mermaid from rushing to the depths of the sea in search of his people, of his underwater palace... that beautiful palace.

Imagery from the memory he had shared with me burned in my brain. Such savagery... it was horrifying. He hadn't told me who it was who had been attacking them, but it certainly hadn't looked like it was anyone from the countries on land. Their weapons had seemed much more adapted to the people in his kingdom, targeting them in a most effective — if horrific — manner.

No country I knew of had those sorts of weapons... not yet, anyway.

Of course, the government doesn't always tell us everything.

Another sobering thought. Was there a chance the government already knew about his people? Had they been responsible for that attack? What sort of a chance had he taken, risking exposure of not just himself, but his people—to come here and find me, and then take me, in a way that was decidedly supernatural.

Anyone could have seen us disappear from my car.

And, several people had seen him in the store... and the coffee house. And he'd checked into that hotel—*and never come and gone from the room like one would expect a person to do.* That had frightened me when I'd realized what he had been doing since he had first checked in there.

What is it about me that is so special, that I am worth risking all of this for?

I felt like he was there in my thoughts... not really saying anything, but subconsciously reminding me of what he'd said after that first afternoon in his hotel room—that I did not see myself very clearly.

Well, how can I? No one has ever shown even remotely the interest in me that you have. Not one man from my past would even compromise with me over stupid little things. Much less risk their very existence, the safety of themself and their people. No one outside of my family—and by family, I mean my mother and my children—has ever thought I was important enough to stick around for, to make compromises for, to give up time or money or even a stupid television show.

"I know, my love."

His internal voice held a tenderness that very nearly made me want to cry. How could the man understand me so well—when we barely knew each other, had barely spent any time together one-on-one... not in bed at any rate.

"I have seen into your very soul, my love. We have been made one. We are bound in ways you cannot seem to comprehend. If only you would let go of your silly human ways, perhaps you could understand."

There was no condescension in his words or his tone. Simply a matter-of-fact statement... one that I somehow knew was correct. Only, I was still loathe to let go of all the things I had learned as a human. Not only did those things bind me to my family in a way he was not really able to understand, I felt there just might be something in those thoughts, feelings and memories that made me the ideal choice for his Queen. He had already said that his advisors had searched the oceans and the land—and I was the best choice of a match for him.

What about me would make me the best match—if it weren't something in me as a person... as a human?

There was a phantom chuckle from somewhere far away. *"Ah, my Queen. One more reason I have given up on attempting to alter your memory."* It wasn't precisely what I'd been getting at. It felt more like he was taking a neutral position in a fight he'd determined he would never win. But I would take it.

Again... a phantom chuckle. *"You see, my love. You do know me better than you think you do. Your human view of marriage may not give you a full understanding of our bond, but it is there as surely for you as it is for me. You know every part of me as intimately as I know you — whether you want to admit it or not."*

Yeah, well. I'll remind you again that I should have been given a choice in the whole thing. And, if I had, I might not be fighting you so much at every turn. Did your Kingly brain think of that?

There was no answer. No chuckle. No thoughts. Just silence. An almost eerie silence.

I found myself focusing, hard, straining to hear his thoughts. I knew he was still there. I could feel his presence in my mind... like always. Had I actually stunned him into silence — such a silence, that he was not only speechless, but unable to even think?

Guess that means I'm right.

Even that got no response from him.

Before I could think anything else his way, my mother cleared her throat — making me realize that I had been having a whole conversation with my Sea King, while she and my daughter waited patiently to talk to me.

What had that looked like to them?

Probably like I'm ignoring them.

She had already been good enough to give me extra time in disappearing. I owed her more than my attention. I owed her an explanation... albeit one I didn't fully have yet, but I would have to tell her something. So, I turned my attention back to them.

"Good morning." I did my best to infuse my voice with enthusiasm. If nothing else, for my daughter's benefit.

"Good morning to you, too." I could see from my mother's expression that I was not off the hook, but that most of what I had to say would need to wait until my daughter was not present—something I agreed with completely.

There was no way I was going to broach any part of the subject of my crazy idea around the children until I had at least run it past Mom... and had a chance to gauge her reaction.

"Did you get an answer... to your question?" She wasn't letting me off the hook completely though.

"Not yet." It was the truth, but I could see that our discussion was not going to end there. She would want to know more about my idea—whether I got the answer I wanted or not. And I had told her I would share. So, I would tell her all about it, whether I wanted to or not.

"Any idea how long before you do?"

I just shook my head, looking from her to where my daughter sat, trying so hard to communicate with my eyes and my body language that we had to wait to have this conversation until little ears were not around.

Whether she got my meaning or not, she let it drop... for the moment at least. "All right. Well, when you do."

"Absolutely. As soon as I know, you'll know."

Fortunately, Cassie chose that moment to demand my attention. Jumping down from where she sat at the table, she rushed over to where I stood and hugged me. Hard. "I missed you, Mommy!"

I returned her hug, waiting until she loosened her grip a little and then leaning down to wrap my arms tightly around her. As I did, it occurred to me how much she had grown recently. Another growth spurt or two and I would no longer need to bend. She would be as tall as me—and then, before long, she would likely be taller.

She snuggled into the hug, content in the knowledge that she was my little girl and I was her mommy and all was right with her world.

Yes, I would definitely have to run the whole idea past my mother before bringing it up to Cassie... and Dylan.

No matter what, it would be a difficult conversation to have. With that in mind, I hugged Cassie a little tighter.

She held on for another few seconds, but then the impatience of youth got the better of her. She let go and waited for me to let go before saying, "I think I'm gonna go read awhile."

Whether from the fear that I would soon lose her... one way or another—or simply from the normal feelings that swamped me almost daily as a mother over how quickly time was passing, I was unexpectedly overwhelmed with emotion. I could only nod as she ran off to get her book from her bedroom.

"Well, now that she's gone..."

The bluntness of her words did not surprise me as they might have once. They did, however, help me to shake off the melancholy feelings that had taken hold of me with Cassie's departure. I turned toward my mother with a half laugh, but smothered it as soon as I saw the seriousness of her expression.

This was not the time.

I looked directly at her, knowing it would reassure her that I was hiding nothing. Not that it really mattered. Most of my life, she'd been able to see past any lies I tried to feed her. "What I said before is the absolute truth. I asked him, but he hasn't given me an answer yet."

"All right. What was the question you asked? And why did you have to rush off to ask it only seconds after the man left?"

I couldn't help but notice she'd said left—as if he had walked out the door, gotten into a car and driven away. Clearly, she was struggling with the obvious supernatural activities she was witnessing. Would it drive her over the edge for me to actually tell her what I had asked him about? And, given that, what were the chances she would simply refuse to deal with it all, delaying my chance to ask the children their thoughts on it in the process?

Would I be better off not telling her exactly what I had asked? Could I fool her? I'd never been a very good liar. She would likely see right through even a half-truth. And then where would we be?

"Well?" She pushed.

It was no surprise. It was what she did. She had very little patience when it came to waiting for something from anyone else.

To say that I was saved by the bell, or rather by the ring, might have been a bit much, but it certainly felt that way when the all-too familiar tune that was specifically programmed for the children's father began ringing from inside my purse.

Since I was already looking at my mother, I saw her roll her eyes... grit her teeth, and then nod a little bit dismissively.

She had never liked Neal, not from day one. She hadn't told me until it was already too late that she'd never wanted me to marry him. By then, I had been expecting Dylan. She'd told me when we were in the hospital, where she had taken me when my vomiting was so intense I couldn't keep anything down. It was serious enough that the doctor feared I would lose the baby if they couldn't put a stop to it.

Just after that—and only because I'd never really told anyone everything that went on in the house I lived in with my husband—I had been diagnosed with intense anxiety, and prescribed three different medicines to help me make it to my actual delivery date. They had very nearly put me on bed rest, only I had known that it wouldn't be feasible. It wouldn't stop my anxiety. It wouldn't help at all.

Mom had stepped in, moved in and taken over caring for me for the remainder of my pregnancy.

Neal had left and went on the road to train for his next big climb.

Mom hadn't minded. Once he had left, she and I had taken our time painting the room we'd picked out as the nursery. We put together furniture and shopped for clothes, diapers, a car seat—all the things we would need for the little one.

Neal had eventually shown up... not at the hospital, but at home... a week after Dylan had made his appearance. He'd stayed with us for exactly a month before he'd left again... to train for his next big climb.

Over the next few years, I nearly left him twice before finding out I was expecting Cassie, at which point mother had insisted I leave him, especially when I had tripped over the climbing gear he had left laying on the floor beside the bed—on my side, and angled in such a way, she'd been certain he'd done it on purpose.

Since there was no way to prove he had been trying to hurt me—and only after the doctor had assured me the baby was one-hundred percent fine—I had decided to take the easy way out and asked for a divorce.

Since I had no grounds—that I could prove

anyway—other than irreconcilable differences, I got a small amount of child support and nothing else. He sold the house and gave me the twenty-five percent his lawyer grudgingly allowed. He sold me my car for about half what he'd paid for it—only after learning he would get no more from it anywhere else. It wasn't surprising really, since it smelled like baby poop and vomit in several places.

And full custody of the children. That was the only thing he didn't fight me on. The lawyers had both agreed that his busy travel and training schedule did not lend itself to shared custody. He was content to have visitation... not that he took advantage of even a quarter of it. The children saw their father when he decided he wanted to see them, and usually with almost no notice.

I had taken what little I could—and my children—and escaped, feeling blessed just to have my freedom back.

And for years, I had not dated. I had barely looked at another man. Exactly three times since, I had been asked out on a date. Since I'd had a marginal interest... and all three times had been spaced far enough apart that I was beginning to feel a bit lonely, I had said yes to each one.

Not one of them had asked for a second date.

And, until the Sea King had whooshed his way into my life, I'd pretty much given up on the idea of ever having a real romance or a marriage again.

Still... he was the children's father, biologically anyway. So, I pulled out the phone, walked toward the living room, and answered.

"Hello, Neal."

"Hey, Kelsey. You remember that fair I took you to on our third date." Not a question. A statement. *Just like him.*

"Yes, I remember." I waited.

"They're having it early this year. Something about the weather or double booking or something. I don't know."

"O... K..." I waited for him to get to the point. If he was about to ask me out, he was in for the shock of his life.

"I was thinking it might be fun for the kids." *Ah.* Now I was beginning to understand.

"I'm sure it would." I wasn't about to make it easy on him. I'd been around this loop too many times.

"So, I was thinking I would take them. I'm in town for a few days and thought it'd be nice to see them." Again, no preamble. No asking if we had plans. No admitting it was last minute and totally out of the blue. Just his timing, his ideas, his plans and his wants.

"I'm sure they would love that."

"Great. I'll pick them up tomorrow afternoon."

"Just for the evening or do you want them for a few days?" He waited a humming thirty seconds before he answered.

"Well, yeah, but don't they have school?" Clueless. Absolutely clueless. *Always was.*

"It's June, Neal." My voice was flat, but really, how difficult was it to remember they were out of school in the summer? He'd been a kid himself once. Did he really not remember when they'd taken a summer break?

"Oh, yeah. Ok. Well, let's just see how the evening goes first." Something about his hesitation made me think he was hiding something. What... I couldn't imagine, but then... I really didn't care enough to worry about it overmuch.

"That works." Knowing full well there was not even a chance of his wanting them for even an overnight.

In the past, when he'd come breezing into town, I would have taken the chance, packed them clothes and overnight bags for a few days stay with their dad. Now I didn't even bother. Even when he wanted to see them for a weekend, it usually only lasted a day before he brought them right back home, making excuses about forgetting he had to be in Colorado or Nepal for some training session or other.

His climbing had always come first, before me, before the children, before anyone or anything else in his life.

His mother had been all for it, proud of the accomplishments her only son had made. He'd been interviewed by every magazine that had anything to do with climbing, twice by TIME, multiple interviews in big New York papers. He was in at least a dozen climbing halls of fame or excellence.

He had a fancy plaque at the base camp of Everest, listing his times from both ventures and that one of those times he'd climbed without oxygen.

But his children, their accomplishments. I was the one who displayed those plaques and trophies, all of the ballet shoes Cassie had outgrown, the shiny little league trophies Dylan had brought home, the mitt he'd used until it literally fell off his hand during a game. I had all of those things. I displayed them around the house. I had pictures on every single wall of the children, of me with them, of us with my mother.

Each child had a picture of their father. Dylan kept his on the nightstand beside his bed. Cassie kept hers in the bottom of a drawer—and only then because I'd caught her every time she tried to throw it out, and made her put it back in her room.

She didn't believe me when I said one day she might appreciate having a picture of her father. But she'd finally stopped trying to throw it away. It rested, face-down at the bottom of her bottom drawer in the tall chest she'd inherited when Mom had finally broken down and bought new bedroom furniture.

"I'll have them ready." Thankfully, I was working short weeks over the summer, only three days a week —and the following day was one I had off. I would be there to warn them when I heard Neal's car pull in. They really didn't need to know before then. Otherwise, they'd both get annoyed when he showed up hours late.

If he showed up at all.

"Yeah. Great. I'll be there around noon." I knew what that meant. He'd show up about four... maybe six or seven.

"Sounds good. We'll see you then."

"Yeah. Bye." And, just like that, he hung up. No chatting. No asking how they'd been in the ten months since he'd seen them. Nothing.

Not that I was surprised. I was used to it by now. I'd had to be, to be the mediator between him and his children, who he barely saw—and to ward off the negative things Cassie tended to say about him... usually when her brother was feeling especially protective of Neal—and it always ended up with the two of them at each other's throats.

It was tempting to just sink down onto the sofa, put off returning to the kitchen for another few minutes, put off my mother. Not that it would do me any good. She would be waiting... however long I tried to delay.

So, with a sigh, I walked back into the kitchen.

"So, he wants to see the children on short notice again." Like Neal, she didn't ask a question—just stated fact.

"Yup." I was too tired now to play games, worn out by this continuous dance we played with his

231

relationship with his children.

"Well, that should make things interesting." She sounded far too smug, though her words confused me.

"I'm not sure I know what you mean." As I said it, I dropped onto a stool on the other side of the kitchen bar she was leaning on, her hands cradling a cup of tea she hadn't been holding when I'd come home.

"I mean, your mysterious male visitor from wherever he's from. He will likely meet your ex. Won't that be fun?" She was laughing now, distracted by the scenario she'd obviously concocted where Nicholas met Neal—and things were certainly going to be interesting if they did meet.

How would I explain Nicholas to Neal? How would I explain Neal to Nicholas? What would he do to the man whose role in my life I had mostly downplayed until now—if he figured out exactly what our relationship had been like?

Even more frightening... was the chance that he already knew. Yes, I had said very little, but he could read my thoughts as easily as most people read a book. Could he read into my memories as easily? Could he have picked through my thoughts as I'd spoken about him before when telling Nicholas about my past?

"I can't wait to see how this all plays out." My mother chuckled a little as she sipped her tea. She said nothing else about the meeting I'd snuck off to or the question I'd just had to ask Nicholas about... for now, at least.

It wasn't much, but it was a win I would take for the moment.

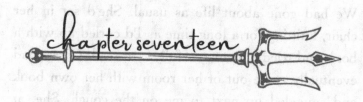

chapter seventeen

TO SAY THAT I WAS NERVOUS THE following afternoon when the time came for Neal's arrival, was the understatement of my life.

Nicholas had been surprisingly silent in my head. No thoughts of his had presented themselves. No comments or questions or answers. Nothing that gave me a clue at all whether he had been listening in on my conversation with the children's father, whether or not he intended to show up and make things complicated, whether he'd picked up on all of the memories that inevitably flooded back to me whenever Neal deigned to call.

Nothing.

I'd paced the floor in my room until I was dizzy. I'd debated getting together clothes for the children, but then changed my mind—and I'd gone back and forth on that point about a hundred times.

My mother had been suspiciously quiet about everything since our conversation the morning before. We had gone about life as usual. She'd sat in her chair, knitting for a long time as I'd curled up with a book and tried... unsuccessfully... to read. Cassie had eventually come out of her room with her own book and snuggled up next to me on the couch. She, at least, had been able to concentrate on her book. I'd watched as she turned the pages, always proud of what a strong reader she was—and marveling that a child born in the midst of a technology boom, still enjoyed reading a paper book... and did so a lot more than she spent time on electronic devices.

Dylan had poked his head out in time for lunch, eaten, and then disappeared back into his room. Sadly, he had never enjoyed reading, like me... or his sister. He preferred immersing himself in the world of make-believe through first person shooter games and the MMRPGs he played online with his friends— none of which I had ever understood the point or the pull of.

It was one of the things Neal was responsible for that, at the time I hadn't realized would be quite the disaster it turned out to be.

When he'd given the game system to Dylan for Christmas, it had seemed like a nice gift, far better than he usually did by the children. It was only later that I found out he had been sponsored by the makers of the gaming system—and had gotten it free of charge as part of the deal. And, since he had absolutely no interest in doing anything that required him to sit still anywhere for more than a few minutes, he had passed it on to Dylan, looking like a hero at the same time.

I'd always wondered if the dollhouse he'd given Cassie at the same time had somehow been a perk of some sponsor or other as well. Though I had no way of finding out—and had only found out about the game system because he mentioned it... not that he had meant to give up any actual credit he'd accumulated by doing such a big thing. But then, to him it was more about showing up and having a gift than where he had actually gotten said gift. He had done work for the company—and they had given him the system. He saw that as something he had paid more than money for, which made it precious in his eyes.

Which also made it no surprise that he'd given it to Dylan instead of Cassie.

She had always felt the lack much more than I'd been comfortable with. I'd done everything I could to soften Neal's dismissive behavior toward her... for as long as I could, but she was entirely too intelligent to miss it. A fact for which I was both thankful for and also regretful of. I could only do so much to repair the damage that Neal himself was doing. And I could never get him to actually understand the consequences of his behavior—not that I expected it to change anything.

It was only one of the reasons I had not mentioned to either child yet, that their father was coming to take them anywhere.

Then I turned—and that all-too-familiar feeling of someone's closeness distracted me from everything else going on in my head at the moment.

Nicholas stood in front of me, blocking me from pacing across the small room yet again. His expression made me wary. There was something in the set of his mouth that told me he was not here to answer the question I had posed to him, but rather to be present when my ex-husband showed up to take the children to the fair.

As I watched, his lips twitched, giving him away... not that my connection with him really even needed that confirmation.

"No. No. No." I started toward him, physically pushing against his chest, even while I reinforced the movement with my thoughts.

"You cannot be here. This is going to be hard enough. I can't. I can't handle you here at the same time as Neal."

Then, when he didn't budge—either physically or

mentally, I tried again. "Please don't make this harder than it is."

"I am not here to cause trouble. I am here for you. I can feel how much you need support. Support that I can give you." He stepped forward, wrapping his large, strong hands around mine. Holding tight. He leaned forward, resting his forehead against mine. "Let me be here for you, my love."

I was not dumb enough to believe that was all he was there for, but the strength in his arms, the closeness of those strong arms, the shelter and protection his very presence offered was too much to ignore in the moment.

I had worked hard to be strong—all on my own—for so long. I had taken on all of the burden. Was it really so wrong to share it—especially since he was not going away? I could feel the determination and resolve in his hands and arms. He was not going to leave. There was nothing I could do. Nothing I could say. He would stay. So, I might as well enjoy having him here.

Fine. OK. I give.

His smile told me he'd known all along that I would give in to him. It worried me that I had, and so easily. Was this a sign of things to come? Would I be the one to give in on everything?

The noise he made then took me completely by surprise, as did the sudden lack of warmth as he stepped back. When I looked up to see what had made him move, his expression had changed drastically.

What? What is it?

"It is you. Will you be the one to give in on everything?"

Yes? And? I nodded absently, clearly missing whatever it was he was reacting to.

"It is a ridiculous question."

Um... what am I missing? How exactly is it a ridiculous question?

"It is a ridiculous question because in the time I have known you, this is the first time that you have given in on anything where I am concerned."

"That is so not true." I spoke quietly, not quite prepared for the rest of the family to know he was here, but I did my best to infuse my words with strength, with intensity. The confusion came all on its own, adding a strange twist to my statement.

"That is how you choose to see things."

"How I choose? What is this crap? No. I'm not choosing to see things any certain way." When I realized I was talking louder... and where the subject of our conversation was going, I switched to non-verbal speech.

Might I remind you that you took me away without my permission or consent. You changed me, made it so that I can no longer live the nice, normal life I've worked so hard to build. You married me without my even knowing it. You took away all of my memories of my life, my family, my children. When I did manage to remember and figure out how to get away from you, you came after me—and you haven't stopped coming. You had your way with me in bed. And, so far, you're getting your way in everything else too. How exactly have I not given in on absolutely everything up to this point?

"You are still here."

I rolled my eyes at the absurdity of his words before answering.

That's it. Really.

He didn't have to answer. I could see the truth of what I was saying in his face. He really believed what he was saying. I shook my head. How had I gotten here—to this point in my life? It had taken six years to re-gain my freedom from one obnoxious jerk. Or, most of it anyway.

And now I was at another man's mercy. Was this destined to be my life, then?

Before I could think anything else—or the stubborn Sea King could... or else push his thoughts into my head, my mother's voice sounded from the living room.

"He's here."

I turned toward the door, steeling myself with a deep breath before dealing with what I knew was coming. Every visit with his children, Neal started out being a nice guy. But, before he left with the children, the nice guy disappeared—and I had to deal with the same obnoxious jerk I'd left all those years ago—for at least a few minutes.

Those strong arms cam around my waist from behind, tightened around me in a gesture that was part hug, part a reminder of his offer to give me the support I needed. He held tight, the warmth from his body—not the supernatural charm kind of heat—seemed to wrap around me as well. It was like a warm, cozy blanket that seeped into my pores and then into my bones, so that he was connected with me physically at a deeper level.

After a few more seconds of basking in his warmth and strength, I took another deep breath, let it out slowly and reached for the doorknob.

And stopped, just as my hand touched it.

The glint of an enormous diamond was winking back at me from the finger that would tell everyone exactly who the Sea King was to me now. And, it had not been there before. I knew it.

"You do not like it, my love?"

That is not the point and you know it.

"How would I know it?"

Well, let's see... I knew my tone was sarcastic—and I truly hoped he could read that as easily as he could read everything else in my head. *Because you can read my thoughts. Duh.*

He said nothing. Thought nothing. Only continued to hold tight to me, though there certainly seemed to be a smugness in his grip now that hadn't been there before. Or maybe I just hadn't wanted to notice it before.

This is because Neal is here, isn't it?

"This is because it is time I showed everyone that you are my wife — and that I am your husband. Why is that wrong? Should we not show everyone how much we mean to each other? Is that not the reason humans wear wedding rings — to show their love outwardly to everyone they meet..."

His logic was ridiculously sensible — and his conclusions might be right for most married couples. But it was not the case with us. And this was not the way I wanted to tell my children that I was married... to a man who controlled the oceans... to a man who wanted to take me back underneath those oceans... far away from them.

However, I also knew this was not a fight I was going to win. He'd obviously used his water power to put it on my finger. No... not it... them. Looking closer, I could see that there was an enormous diamond ring, but also a gem encrusted band behind it. When I held my hand up to look at it, I could see all of the stunning colors of gems woven into the intricate criss-crossing shapes of what looked like metal on the band. It truly was beautiful. When I looked closer at the diamond ring, I could see the repetition of those shapes and gems woven into the thinner band that held the ridiculously large diamond.

There was no denying their beauty — and there was

no surprise that he wanted me to wear them. *But did he have to choose right now to put them on my hand?*

I didn't have to ask—and he didn't have to answer, either out loud or in my thoughts. I knew the why. And I knew he would just put the rings right back on if I pulled them off. So, I squared my shoulders and took hold of the knob again, opening the door this time without looking back down at my hand.

I walked down the hall, Nicholas right behind me. I could still feel the warmth radiating off him, almost like he was doing something to make it reach out to me. It was comforting, but also distracting—which was probably at least one of the reasons for it.

"Nonsense. I am merely trying to help you."

Yeah. If you were only trying to help me, you would take these rocks off and not be right here flaunting your presence in front of my ex-husband.

He didn't respond to either of my comments. I hadn't really expected him to. I squared my shoulders and moved further down the hall, pausing at Cassie's room, knocking brightly on her door frame. Her door was wide open.

She must have already seen me coming down the hall—or else heard her grandmother's voice and wondered at who was here because she bounced into the doorway as soon as my knuckles landed on the wood.

"Who's here?" She must have noticed Nicholas then—and she must have thought that was who Mom had meant, because she squealed and started to move around me before stopping, pouting a little. "Oh pooh. I missed the watery entrance."

"See. She likes me." I could almost feel Nicholas gloating behind me.

She's twelve. And she's not the one you have to get to like you, mister. I tried to make my voice sound harsh, but there was just such a joyful tone to his words in my head... like a little boy who has discovered someone he thought hated him actually likes him. I might not want to give him an inch, but he had a point. Cassie did like him. Dylan was impossible to judge, but he hadn't shown any signs that he didn't like Nicholas.

Mother was the only one who seemed to dislike the Sea King—and I had a feeling her like or dislike was more about what he had done to me... and the very real possibility that he would eventually take me somewhere far away from my family and keep me there.

Something I would have to deal with... but not today.

chapter eighteen

BEFORE I COULD TELL CASSIE THAT Nicholas was not who her grandmother had been talking about, Neal came walking down the hall.

"Hey, there's my little Cassie. You got a hug for daddy?"

At the sound of her father's voice, Cassie's smile disappeared. Her shoulders slumped. The light went out of her eyes—and she looked more like she wanted to run away and hide than hug him.

I wanted to cringe at the change in my sweet Cassie's expression and posture, but I steeled myself against my natural reactions. Now was certainly not the time.

Later

Later, I could deal with her reactions. After he'd gone—when it was just her and I. We could talk then.

"I do believe I understand now what you meant about the mother bear instinct."

The comment was so far beyond what I had come to expect from him, I very nearly laughed. Again, I caught myself before I could show the totally inappropriate response to the situation at hand. The last thing I wanted to do was explain to Neal why I was suddenly laughing when he asked his daughter for a hug.

Cassie looked up at me with a question in her eyes, pleading with me to give her some out, some way she did not have to pander to the man who barely tolerated her existence... and then, only when he felt like it.

Unfortunately, I didn't have any. I shrugged slightly and smiled at her, trying to remind her with just my eyes and smile that she was a bigger person than he was... would ever be.

Fortunately, she was the bigger person, the one of them who was far more mature—in so many ways. So, instead of pouting and refusing to hug him, she turned and held out her arms.

"Hi, Dad."

I wondered somewhat absently whether Neal noticed his daughter's behavior or if he was just so stuck on himself, it passed him right by. She went to him, but she didn't run or bounce or squeal—like she just had for Nicholas.

How did he miss that? How did he not see the truth behind it? How did it not break his heart as much as it did mine to see how distant his own daughter felt from him?

"Because he is self-centered and narcissistic."

Again, I was tempted to laugh. Not just at how unexpected his comment was. It wasn't really. But at the parallels that were right in front of him—and, yet he missed them all.

Oh, you're one to talk.

He, of course, didn't miss a beat.

"My desire for you to join me has nothing to do with my own wants and needs."

Nothing? You sure about that?

I thought back to our last night together, fixing the images in my mind—knowing he would see them as clearly as I did.

"Would you prefer I did not enjoy our time together? Would that somehow make my motives less selfish?"

I should have known there was no arguing with him.

"Is Dylan in his room?"

Of course. Having gotten his hug, he was ready to move on to the favorite child. His son.

"Yes. He's playing video games—as usual." I didn't bother to disguise the loathing in my tone. He wouldn't pick up on it anyway. He had never seen the danger in giving his son something that caused him to be closeted in his room for hours at a time, only coming out when we insisted.

"He should have more care of his children. Does he not see that you are only concerned for their well-being?"

Nope. He only sees what he wants — and how good it makes him feel to be the good guy.

I was a little bit surprised that Nicholas saw the narcissistic behaviors in Neal so clearly. Maybe there was hope for him yet.

Maybe.

"I do not understand why you insist on questioning my motives in this. I am trying very hard to align myself with your worry for the children you have chosen over me."

Well, that would be one reason I question your motives — right there in your own words. I am not choosing them over you. They are my children. They are a part of me. I cannot leave them behind and go off to some strange underwater kingdom — no matter how much you might want me to. You do not understand and I have no other way to explain it to you.

I looked straight ahead as I spoke — even though I really wanted to turn and smack him soundly.

Neal hadn't even seemed to notice him.

A fact that annoyed me more than his insistence to stay. Neal was often self-centered, but not to the point of ignoring an entire human being. So, unless Nicholas had done something to make himself invisible to my ex-husband...

"Why would I need to hide from such a man—a man who is more interested in himself than his beautiful wife and adoring children?"

Laying it on a bit thick maybe, but yeah. You have a point. And I'm not his wife. I'm your wife. As you continue to remind me.

I didn't have to turn around to know Nicholas was smiling at my acknowledgment that I was *his* wife. When his arms tightened around me just a bit more, I knew that what I had said pleased him more than anything I had said.

Still... I couldn't help but notice that the more I compared Neal to Nicholas, the more weaknesses and flaws I saw in the man who was my ex-husband.

You wouldn't have anything to do with that, would you?

No response.

And, before I had time to press, Neal was back in the hallway, Dylan in tow, Cassie walking slowly behind them and looking quite glum about something.

I knew she never enjoyed visiting with her father, but I had really thought she would be excited about the fair. It was something fun that I had taken them to multiple times over the years. She might not have the same sort of fun with her father and her brother, but there was still plenty of fun to be had there.

Even so, I waited until the three of them had stopped in front of me before I asked.

"So, the fair?"

"Yeah. Dad told me all about it. It sounds amazing!" Dylan sounded more excited than he had in months—since the last time Neal had swooped into town unexpectedly and dropped in to visit.

Cassie just rolled her eyes. And... her emotions were pretty much exactly where they had been the last time her father had dropped in unexpectedly and dragged her somewhere she really had no interest in going. Somewhere he wanted to go, because he didn't really care whether or not she wanted to go... or whether or not she wanted to spend time with him. He just wanted what he wanted.

Just like he always had.

"Well, you guys have fun."

Neal was already turning and heading for the door. Dylan was right beside him. Cassie dragged behind, looking over her shoulder at me, begging me with her eyes to let her stay.

I wanted to stop them. I wanted to tell Neal she needed to stay. So many things I wanted in that moment—to tell Neal he didn't need to drag her with them just to prove he could. But I couldn't.

I knew what it would mean. Another court battle. And, even though he really didn't want his children with him all the time, he did want to hurt me, which would mean he would find a way to take them away from me if I pushed him too hard.

And what if I lost control of my abilities in the courtroom? What if someone found out about me—about all the crazy changes? I would not only lose my children. I would be locked away somewhere, forever... or until the Sea King broke me out—and endangered himself and his people in the process.

Not a good idea.

"I would not let him take your children away from you."

That's nice to say, but you can't really do anything about that. This is very much a human thing. You can't just snap your fingers and make it all go away. I wish you could, but it just doesn't work that way.

"And if it did?"

What does that mean?

I was almost afraid to ask, but I had to know what he was getting at.

"It's nothing. You need not worry about a thing. I will take care of you. I will take care of this."

What do you mean? What are you going to do?

No answer.

He said nothing—and this time I did try to find the answers in his mind, but whatever it was he was hiding was locked up so tightly, I couldn't get to it—which worried me more than a little.

"Fine." I shook me head at the ridiculousness of the situation as I headed for the door. I might not be able to make Neal let Cassie stay, but I could at least wave to her as they drove away.

They had just closed the door when I reached it, With a slightly ironic laugh, I pulled it open and followed them out. Trust Neal to think that I would have no interest in seeing my children off for however long he decided he would take them.

Dylan was already opening the door of Neal's fancy car. Neal was right behind him, reaching for the door handle on the driver's side. Cassie was dragging behind—and, when she heard the door close behind me, she turned and ran back to wrap her arms around me.

"Do I have to go, Mommy? Please don't make me. Please?"

The gloomy tone in her voice made me want to snatch her up and promise she didn't have to go anywhere. But, since I knew I couldn't do that, I untangled her arms, squatted down to her level, and then hugged her. Her arms came around me tightly again, holding like she never wanted to let go.

"Sweetie, I know you don't remember, but you used to have fun at this fair with your dad."

"I don't remember. And I don't wanna go. Come on, Mom. You know they'll never miss me."

She was right. Mostly. They would never miss her —not really. But, Neal would use it against her... and against me.

"They would miss you. And you'd miss out on the

fun. Come on. Rides. Cotton candy. Hot dogs. What's not to love? You're going to have fun." As I said it, I slipped some money into her pocket, knowing that Neal would spend all sorts of money on Dylan. But he would only spend the least he could get away with on her.

"There. Now you can get what you want... not just what your dad decides to get you."

She didn't let go.

After several more seconds of hugging her, Neal called out for her to hurry up. So, I gently untangled her arms again.

"Come on now. The faster you go, the faster it's all over and you can come back home." I laughed as I said it—and, luckily, she did too.

"I love you, Mommy!"

I hugged her again, really tight, for just a second before letting go again. "I love you too, kiddo. Now go have fun."

"Ok. I'll try. See you later, Nicholas." And then she turned and moved over to the car, walking more slowly than I'm sure Neal liked. I didn't rush her.

I hadn't realized Nicholas had followed me out. I should have. I usually felt his presence. It should have worried me, but I had more important things on my mind at the moment.

I watched as she got into the car and closed the door behind her. I watched as she buckled her seat belt—and Neal started the car and started backing down the driveway. I waved as they backed out of the driveway. I kept waving as they pulled away, down the road, away from me. Cassie was the only one who kept waving as they drove out of sight.

Then I just stood there, watching absently... the last place they had been.

My heart broke for my sweet baby girl. It might have felt out of proportion to some people. Goodness knew there were people who thought I was ridiculous... like Cassie was ridiculous for not wanting to visit with her dad. But I knew how it felt to spend time with someone who cared absolutely nothing for you... someone who was only using you as a tool to make themselves feel better, or worse... someone who was using you as a tool to hurt someone else.

That was Neal. He had no interest in visiting with his daughter, but she came with her brother—and, taking her away hurt me... which was the real reason he did it.

I wanted to find some way to give Cassie a break from being her dad's tool to hurt me, but there was nothing I could do.

Not a single thing.

How long I stood there, watching the spot where Neal's car had disappeared, I lost track of. But, when I finally did turn and take a step back toward the door, I was surprised all over again to see Nicholas standing there.

Had he been there all this time?

Why hadn't I known it?

What was he doing, that I couldn't feel his presence?

There were no answers—not from him, not in my own mind, in the place deep down where all the answers should be, that place where all of the knowledge that had come with these new abilities had tucked itself.

Nothing.

He was doing something to block himself off from me—and the knowledge inside my own head had no idea what it was.

I wasn't going to wait to see what it was. I was going to go inside and find a movie to distract myself... and have a good cry. I walked back toward the door, toward him.

"Well, I'm going to go inside and do what I usually do when they're gone. You're welcome to join me."

With that, I stepped around him and went inside the house, reaching back to shut the door... but, he beat me to it. He'd followed me inside.

Of course. The thought was only a little bitter. I was actually happy not to be alone. Mom had done what she did every time Neal came around—been elsewhere. She couldn't stand him. And she couldn't stand watching him take my children away from me... even if it was only for a few hours. So, she always made herself scarce when he was supposed to come.

She would come back when she was sure he would

be gone again... which meant she wouldn't come back for several hours—until I called or texted her and told her he was gone.

I would have been all alone, if not for Nicholas.

Suddenly, I was actually happy he'd showed up. I wouldn't have to face the next few hours by myself, worrying as I waited... wondering if Neal was being good to Cassie or ignoring her like he usually did.

I could distract myself with Nicholas.

With that in mind, and an unexpected idea popping into my mind, I turned and stepped up to him.

I leaned into his chest, wrapped my arms around him and leaned up to kiss him. When he didn't move, or lean toward me, I reached up with one hand and tugged at his collar until he leaned forward, meeting my lips with his.

It didn't take long for the heat between us to catch him up on my thought process. And then he was kissing me back with a fierceness I hadn't expected.

The next thing I knew, we were tumbling onto my bed. The only question was, had he whooshed us there... or had I?

It was hours before I thought again of the children. We were laying on our sides, facing each other, limbs and sheets tangled up between and around us.

"You know, I hate to break this up, but it's starting to get dark. They could get back anytime now."

Nicholas only leaned in for another kiss, stopping me most effectively from saying more.

I let him kiss me, let myself sink back into the liquid desire we could create between us, let my mind wander as his hands started to move over me again, distracting me.

Then I heard the door close and a distant shout.

"Mom! We're back!"

I scrambled out of the bed and started to search for my clothes. But, before I could find the first item, the water swirled around me — and I was dressed.

"Thanks." For once, I didn't mind the slightly sneaky ability.

He said nothing in return, but when I turned to look back at him, he was gone. "O... K..." It was strange, but I wasn't going to complain.

Then I turned back toward the door — and he was standing in front of me, also fully dressed.

I laughed. "Ok. Yeah."

I didn't take the time to say anything else, not wanting the questions that would come from the children if they saw us both walking out of my bedroom.

It would be bad enough for them to see us both

walk down the hallway, from the direction of my bedroom.

With all of that in mind, I moved quickly to the door of my bedroom, opened it and headed down the hall toward the living room.

Neal was standing in the middle of the living room, hugging Dylan. Cassie was sprawled on the couch, absently picking bits of cotton candy out of a large, plastic bag, watching her brother and father hug, with a slightly strange expression on her face.

I walked into the room, moved right past Neal and Dylan, settling myself on the sofa right next to Cassie, taking the bit of cotton candy she offered me and popping it into my mouth.

It melted on my tongue, just like I remembered from the last time I had gone to the fair with the children.

Neal hadn't taken them—or me—to the fair since we'd been dating. However, I had taken the children multiple times as they were growing up. At least, until they'd outgrown their desire to go to the local fair with their mother, anyway.

"It was fun. Some of it anyway." Cassie spoke softly, her voice laced with surprise, but also more than a little annoyance.

"Which parts were fun?" I felt as if I knew what her answer would be, but I asked the question anyway.

"The parts where I went off on my own." There

was more annoyance coating her voice now. I knew why. I didn't even need to ask.

She hadn't expected to have any fun, but she had gone—mostly because I asked her to. Then Neal had let her go off on her own because he really didn't want to spend any time with her anyway.

I would never have let her go off completely on her own. I started to ask whose idea it had been, but she answered the question before I could ask.

"Yes, it was Dad's idea for me to go off on my own, but don't worry, Mom. I wasn't completely alone. I bumped into a whole group of friends from school—and Dad suggested I go off with them for awhile.

I nodded. "Good thing I made sure you had some money."

I looked at the cotton candy bag in her hands. Surely that wasn't all she had eaten. I wanted to ask, but I hesitated. She was getting older and was beginning to resent my worrying.

Again, she answered me before I could ask. "Don't worry, Mom. We had hot dogs and fries for dinner. I got the cotton candy *after* I had eaten."

I nearly laughed at the extra emphasis she put on the word *after*. She was more grown up—right now— at twelve years old, than her father had ever been. Somehow, she had escaped most of the childish behaviors Neal had passed on to his son.

When she let out a soft sigh, I reached over and wrapped one arm around her, pulling her close up

261

against my side. Perhaps her not having inherited his childishness had something to do with Neal's constant dismissal of her. Or maybe it had nothing to do with that. Maybe she reminded him too much of me—and that made him want to hurt her in ways he had hurt me, with that cold disregard he was so good at. That, along with the constant rejection... plus, in my case the verbal abuse and outright neglect.

It was no wonder she was as normal as she was, loving and open. She was definitely more me than she had ever been like her father. A fact for which I was eternally grateful. In that gratitude, I snuggled her against me a little closer. She leaned in and sighed again, but this time it was one of contentment.

We sat there for several minutes, in a comfortable silence, watching Neal and Dylan talk. They joked and laughed about the evening they'd had. They were completely oblivious to anything else going on around them, anyone else in the room with them.

It was more than a little upsetting.

Then, at some point, possibly some unspoken signal, Neal detached. He told Dylan he had to get going. My guess was he had a date or something.

Maybe his phone buzzed in his pocket and reminded him.

He hugged Dylan one more time and then turned, stopping short after a step in our general direction, looking like a deer caught in headlights. He had completely and totally forgotten his daughter was right here, waiting for his attention.

"Well, come give daddy a hug, sweetheart. I've got to be going."

To her credit, she did get up and go over to Neal. She gave him a hug—albeit a short one. She moved away the moment he let go.

Then he was turning back to his son. "Night, Dylan."

"Night, Dad." And then Dylan was slowly inching backward toward his room.

Cassie stayed where she was as Neal made a final wave to the room in general and then headed for the door.

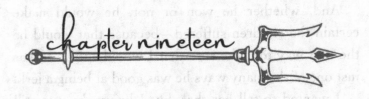

chapter nineteen

ONCE NEAL WAS OUT THE DOOR,
Dylan wasted no time in rushing off to his room... no
doubt to continue playing the video game that had
been interrupted earlier with his dad's arrival.

I let him go with no comments. He had already
talked the evening through with Neal. I'd caught
enough of their conversation to know what all they'd
been up to. I didn't need to hear it again from a teen
who would rather be off doing something else...
anything else.

Cassie, however, turned back to look at me. Her
expression told me she was hurting. Her body

language told me she was angry. I ached for my baby girl. I had pushed her into going with them because it was easier all around, but I had also done it because I knew that whatever slights she received at her father's hand throughout the evening were nothing compared to the torment he would put her through during a court battle.

And, whether he won or not, he would make certain the children suffered—because that would be the best way to make sure that I would suffer. It was just one of the many ways he was good at being a jerk.

I wanted to tell her that, but I knew she was still too young to really understand. I also did not want to make her view of Neal any more disturbing than it already was. She had enough of a tarnished outlook on their relationship as it was.

She flopped down on the couch beside me and threw her arms around me, holding on hard. "Please, don't make me go next time, Mom." Her words were slightly muffled since she'd pulled herself up tightly against me.

I wanted to tell her I wouldn't make her. I wanted to tell her she never had to go anywhere with Neal ever again.

But I knew I couldn't do that.

"I wish I could, baby girl."

She pulled away, her eyes bright with the sting of betrayal.

"Wait." I held up a hand to stop her, distract her,

anything... until I could get this out. "You know I would never do anything to hurt you, right?"

She nodded.

"Then you know how much I wish I could tell you that you never have to go anywhere with Neal again."

She nodded again, but then her head drooped and I could see she understood where I was going with this.

"You know he would make things difficult for us if I tried to keep him from getting what he wants."

"Yeah, I know." Her voice was so small, so broken, it broke my heart right along with hers.

I pulled her back into my arms and squeezed, then rubbed a hand over her back in an attempt to calm her, to soothe her.

"Hey, look at the bright side. He hardly ever takes his scheduled visits. It could be six months before you have to see him again."

She laughed at that. It wasn't her usual, full-bodied laugh, but it was enough to tell me that we were over the worst of this bout of post dad-visit depression.

"Wanna watch a movie?"

"Sure, which one?"

"You pick." I knew which movie she would pick, but I also knew she needed something comforting, familiar, humorous.

So, she went to get the movie and I went to make some popcorn. Then, we snuggled up on the couch and watched our favorite movie of a mean, rude

267

prince and the princess he plotted to kill, ahh'd over the swashbuckling Spaniard, oohed over the rhyming giant, laughed hysterically over the know-it-all—but not really—Sicilian, and gushed over the triumph of true love.

By the end of the movie, I was pleased to feel that the tension had mostly gone out of Cassie's slim shoulders. Although she did snuggle with me for the entire movie. Usually, she would start out sitting next to me, then snuggle when the giant rats showed up, then move away as the bishop started saying things in his oh-so-silly way. This time, she snuggled up before we even hit play—and didn't move away til we heard the back door open.

"I trust he's gone?" Mom called out to us from the kitchen, as she walked through to the living room.

I answered. "Yes." just as Cassie called out a "Yeah." And then we laughed together.

A few seconds later, Mom walked into the living room and saw the credits rolling on a movie she'd probably memorized after all these years—and immediately knew the evening had not gone well. I could see by the look on her face.

I took the opportunity to get Cassie out of the room—before Mom could unload on Neal and get her all upset again. "Cassie, honey, why don't you go brush your teeth and get in your pajamas. I'll come and tuck you in soon."

She pushed herself off the couch and started

toward the bathroom she and her brother shared, but then turned back and threw her arms around me for one more quick hug.

I could almost hear my mother's teeth grinding together in her effort not to say anything until Cassie was out of the room.

And, to her credit, she waited until we could hear water running in Cassie's bathroom before she started talking.

"What did he do this time? Has he not hurt that sweet child enough? When will he ever learn that he can't treat people this way—especially his own children?"

"Mother, you know I don't have any control over how he treats her. If I did, I would never let him within a hundred yards of her. If I had any hope of changing the way he behaves toward people, it would have been while we were married. Now, I'm just a target for him. You know that."

She seethed, but quietly. I could see the struggle it was for her. I'm sure all the times she had listened to me cry over something or other that he had done while we were married still haunted her. She was likely reliving them—maybe every time we heard from Neal. Certainly every time he was mean to me... or Cassie.

"If I thought I had a chance, I would take him back to court, but you know he's got much deeper pockets than we do. That's why he won so spectacularly before." We both knew that I should be receiving much more financial support from him than I was. And, since I hadn't worked during the marriage, I should have gotten some spousal support as well. But his lawyer had been a fancy, high-priced shark, and had torn mine to shreds.

Fortunately, the judge had taken a little bit of pity on us—and she'd awarded a decent amount of child support. If nothing else, it had inspired me to figure out how to do things on my own.

So, I had moved back in with my mother, found a job, and done everything I could to start rebuilding my life.

"Well, at least you got Cassie calmed down—or, at least, it looked that way to me."

I was already nodding, before she finished talking. "I did. Yeah."

Mother gestured toward the television. "Her favorite movie."

"And mine." I added, with a little laugh.

"And how many lines did she quote tonight?"

I looked away before answering. I gathered up the remains of our late-night snack. Then headed to the kitchen. "Only one or two."

"Wow. He really did a number on her this time." When I didn't say anything in return, she went on. "And for how much of the movie was she snuggled up against you?"

I turned to face her then. "All of it. Yeah, I know.

It was bad. He basically went off and left her alone. Fortunately, she ran into some of her friends, so she wasn't alone at the fair all night." I held up a hand when she started to speak.

"Yes, I know precisely how dangerous it was. And I know you're going to suggest we use it to take away his visitation, but just remember, Mom, what a shark he has for a lawyer. I mean, I'm doing ok financially, but I could never afford a shark to match his. And if we take him back to court without a rock solid, smoking gun full of evidence, we will lose. Think about how much worse that could be."

"I wasn't going to say anything about taking him back to court. I was going to suggest we get Cassie a cell phone. That way, when things like that happen, she can call us. At least let us know what's going on. And then, if he leaves her somewhere like that—and she doesn't have friends to hang out with, we can go and get her."

I started to argue, but it wasn't the worst idea. It would likely tick off Neal, but it would be no more than he deserved. And if he left her all alone, and she called me to come and get her, I would be well within my rights to do so.

"It's worth a try."

Mom had opened her mouth—probably to argue against whatever excuse I was about to give her, but she closed it instead. Then, a moment later, opened it again. "Good. I'll start shopping around tomorrow while you're at work."

"Sounds good." I leaned in to hug her.

She hugged me back, pulling me tight up against her—much the same way I had pulled Cassie in close to me earlier. It was nice. It was comforting. A part of me wanted to stay there awhile, snuggle up in that familiar embrace of safety and comfort.

But too quickly, she was pulling away. "You'd better go tuck in your daughter before she comes looking for us."

Laughing a little at that image, I nodded. "Night, Mom."

"Good night, sweetheart."

Then I headed down the front hall to where Cassie's room was. Mom headed to the back of the house where her room was.

Cassie was snuggled up in bed, looking much more normal than I'd expected. She wasn't snuggling her stuffed animals or hiding under the covers like she sometimes did after a visit with Neal. She seemed just fine.

I was glad to see it. The movie had definitely done her well. And she obviously hadn't heard any of my conversation with her grandmother. Or she would be peppering me with questions and wishes about what cell phone she could get.

"Hey, baby girl. I'm here to tuck you in, as promised."

In response, she snuggled down into the covers a

little, holding her arms out for a hug.

I leaned over her bed and folded myself into the hug. I was glad to feel her shoulders and body were completely relaxed. There were no lingering signs of tension. She didn't cling either. She just hugged me— and then let me go with a happy sigh.

I wanted to take it at face value. Be happy that she was doing so much better. However, the mother within me had to be sure.

"I'm glad you're feeling so much better, honey. The movie helped, huh..."

She didn't respond at all like I expected her to. She screwed up her face a little as she slowly sat up. "The movie was great, but what do you mean feeling better, Mommy? I'm fine. I've been fine. Did something happen with you? Are you ok?"

Right away, I was concerned. Why was she acting like nothing had been wrong? Was she avoiding the topic for some reason? Was she playing a game of some sort? There was nothing I could think of that actually made sense.

"No, sweetheart. I'm fine."

She relaxed visibly. "Oh good. I was starting to worry about you, mom."

I was really starting to worry about her. "Ok, honey. You know... maybe you weren't as upset earlier as I thought. I was only saying how happy I am that you're ok. I know your visits with Neal are never easy."

If her behavior before had worried me, her next words took it to a whole other level.

"I don't know what you mean, Mommy. Who is Neal? Mom, who is that? When did we visit with him?"

I watched her face for some sort of sign that she was kidding... or else just being a little bit weird about her father. There was nothing. No sign that she was kidding. Just a look of complete confusion.

How could she not remember her father's name?

From somewhere far, far away came an all-too-familiar voice, floating into my head like a feather... a big, black, feather of steel and spikes—doing its damage in every square inch of my life. *My love, what are you doing? You are only going to upset her—asking her about someone she doesn't know.*

What exactly do you mean—someone she doesn't know? How could she not know her father?

"I thought this was what you wanted. You said as much, more than once—and in more than one way." His cool, clear calm logic made me want to scream.

What. Did. You. Do?!?

I knew there was an edge to my mental voice. I didn't even try to disguise or soften it. He had done something—something he hadn't run by me or warned me about. And, it was affecting my child, my sweet little girl. How dare he!

"This is what you wanted, my love. Now everything

will be better. You will not have to worry about Neal or your children with him anymore."

I still wanted to scream, but not while sitting with my sweet daughter. I blocked out the arrogant Sea King for a moment and turned my attention back to Cassie.

"You know what, sweetheart. I'm thinking of something else. I'm so sorry. I guess I'm more tired than I realized. Maybe I'm still kind of stuck in a fictional world, you know what I mean..." And I laughed, trying to make it sound like I was just confused or being silly or something.

She didn't look convinced, but she must have decided to let it go because she smiled and sat back. "I know what you mean, Mommy. I'm really tired, too. Guess I should get to sleep."

Then she snuggled back into her covers with another small sigh. "Night, Mommy. Love you."

I leaned over and kissed her forehead, smoothing back the hair that had curled down over her beautiful eyes as I did. "Good night, sweetie. I love you, too. So much."

I stood, moved over to the door, reached for the light switch, watching her the whole time—just in case she was playing a game or being silly—even though, deep down I knew she was not. This was *his* doing. I clicked off the light just as Cassie turned over on her side, waving at me a little as I took a step out into the hallway.

As I moved down the hall, the anger seethed within me. He had done something to her memory... like he had done something to mine. He had taken something from her. The question was how much. How many of her memories had he taken? He said she didn't know Neal. How could he have taken just memories of Neal without taking others? And why? Why would he do this!?! The urge to scream was almost too much now.

OOH! How dare he do something creepy—and then go away, leaving me to deal with the fallout!

"You are the one who wanted to be their mother, without any interference from me, remember?" And now he was throwing my thoughts back at me...

Why was I surprised?

And why did he have to keep saying he had done it for me? Yes, I might have thought about what he'd apparently done, but it had been one of those things an ex-wife thinks about her ex-husband. It was not something I would ever have actually done... or tried to do... or been able to do before I'd had access to the incredible Queen of all the oceans powers.

The thought of those powers gave me an idea. Before I could talk myself out of it, I reached out, found where he was, and transported myself to him.

We were in his hotel suite, of course. Standing in the middle of the living room. There was a mug of some sort of hot liquid sitting on the small table next to the chair right behind him. There was steam rising lazily out of the cup. He had to have been sitting there just a few seconds ago.

I refused to be swayed by his gentlemanly behavior. He had done something to my children, something that would have untold effects on them — maybe forever.

See, this is one of those times where... one: you need to know that what a person thinks does not always align with what they want or what is actually ok to do... and two: you shouldn't just assume you know what a person wants, whether you can read their mind or not. You should ASK before you do something that changes a person's life forever!

He said nothing. He did nothing. Simply stood there, looking like the arrogant Sea King. There was no hint of shame anywhere in him... not in his posture, his expression or his thoughts. Could he actually be convinced that what he'd done was a good thing?

How? Tell me how this is your answer to everything? And why? I mean, is it just easier to get a person to do what you want them to once you've wiped away everything you don't like about their past? You discard whatever is in the way in their life and then you can... what... have your way with them?

Is that how you keep your kingdom in line? You just erase what you don't like in your subject's lives... in their past... in their personalities?

I stumbled backward when the first crash of lightning hit the ground only a few feet from where we were standing.

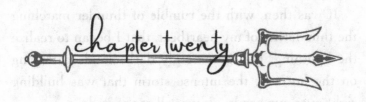

chapter twenty

I WAS SHOCKED TO SEE THAT WE WERE no longer in his suite. We were standing by the water... on the beach... by an ocean. I don't know how I knew, but somehow I knew it was the pacific— which was on the opposite coast from where I lived. Had he done this or had I? Whoever had done it... we had somehow traveled thousands of miles in a moment—a trip that had taken place so quickly, I hadn't even noticed the transfer.

Not even a second later, another bolt hit—in almost the exact same spot, so close I could feel the electricity snap and sizzle in the air around us. It completely distracted me from my wonderings, pulling my attention to what was going on around us.

Thunder rolled right above us, at such a volume and intensity, it blocked out every other sound, building until my ears were ringing. Then, with almost no break, it started again, and it actually sounded even louder than the first rumble.

It was then, with the rumble of thunder matching the thundering of my heartbeat, that I began to realize the lightning, the increasingly dark clouds gathering on the horizon, the intense storm that was building right over our heads—it was all connected.

And, it was somehow connected to me, to my anger, to my frustration, to the emotional roller coaster I was on with knowing what I knew about the stupid Sea King and what he had done.

Was I doing this? Was I somehow making the storm? Was this a part of the stupid abilities he had given me... abilities that I'd never wanted?

I didn't have to ask. I could see the answer as plainly as the self-satisfied smirk on his face. And with it, I realized the storm perfectly mirrored the sudden urge for violence that was building within me.

What had he done to me?

"Why is it always me!" I shouted, though there was no one but him around to hear me—not that anyone could have heard me with the pounding of the storm, the almost constant rumbling of thunder and the wind that was whipping everywhere with such speed, it was beginning to frighten me.

He said nothing. Just continued to stand there in front of me with that stupid smirk on his ridiculously handsome face.

The next lightning bolt hit between us, inches from his feet. I could feel the hair on the back my neck standing up. There was electricity snapping all around us—and he just stood there with that same stupid smirk.

I knew I needed to calm down. I knew I needed to figure out how to stop this. I knew I didn't want anyone to get hurt. But, at the same time, I wanted him to know just a tiny bit of the pain he had caused... a fraction of what he had brought into my life... and my children's lives. I also knew he was not just some ordinary human. With my luck, a lightning bolt wouldn't even hurt him.

And, with the next strike, he proved me right. The lightning came down, so incredibly fast—and instead of moving or using his own abilities to stop it, he just stood there.

Unbelievably, when it hit... he held out his hand... and it struck right in the middle of his open palm. There was a blinding light as it hit, a frightening amount of sparks, and then... nothing.

The lightning fizzled out—and left behind not a single scorch mark or piece of evidence that it had ever touched him.

He just stood there... that smirk still firmly in

place... maybe even a little bigger than it had been. But, otherwise, not a single shred of evidence that he had been hit with something that would have completely destroyed anyone else. I had to admit to myself then, it was a little frightening—to see how powerful he was.

I took a step back. And then another. And then another—until I was several feet from him. And then I stood there—and stared at him.

Above me, the storm was blowing itself out. The clouds were dissipating. The thunder rumbled still, but it was getting more and more calm. The wind that had been howling, was now whispering through the trees and around the ends of my hair. The rain that had been pelting, drenching the ground around us, was barely a mist now.

And... somehow... he was completely dry, and completely untouched. Not even a hair looked to be out of place.

I couldn't take it. I turned, started walking down the beach, away from him—and I must have tapped into my abilities without even thinking—because, the next step I took was onto my bedroom floor. Another transfer so fast, I hadn't even noticed it.

I moved over to my bed and sank down onto the mattress. This was getting a little crazy. Lord knew I felt crazed. Everything in my head was spinning.

I was traveling thousands of miles in a blink. My daughter didn't remember her father. My mother was still waiting for an explanation about what I had asked Nicholas—an answer he still hadn't given me.

And he was still playing with my life whenever and however he saw fit. It was enough to drive anyone to drink. Alcohol, not water. It certainly made me want to scream. And cry. And hit something. And throw something. And to find a way to make it all just stop.

Not more than a second later, I felt more than heard the whoosh of water that would have brought him into my room.

I didn't look up. I just stared at the floor in front of where his feet were. The old, worn, faded, mostly clean carpet that probably should have been replaced years before was such a contrast with his overly shiny, obviously expensive shoes.

Oddly enough, I found myself wondering why the King of the Seas would have such expensive shoes. Had he charmed them out of some salesperson or simply whooshed them out of the store with his abilities? How else would he have gotten them? And was that the reason he wasn't worried about the people in the hotel noticing that he hadn't come and gone—because they didn't remember him checking in? Maybe he'd made it so they didn't even remember the room he was in existed... until he wanted room service or housekeeping.

I could not imagine him doing any cleaning himself —and no one else had been there in those rooms... other than me.

Or had he removed treasure from some of the millions of shipwrecks littering the bottom of the sea and traded that in for some of our money... or rather, a lot of our money?

His shoes didn't offer up any answers. And, neither did he. I could have easily looked into his mind and found the answers, but I found I really didn't care all that much. It was just a random train of thought wandering through my mind as I tried to deal with what he had done this time—and how absolutely insane it was making me feel.

"I was attempting to help you. I did not think you would be so unhappy with my actions."

His words had the ring of truth—and I knew he was being truthful, but it was not because he thought what he'd done was wrong. It was really only because I was angry.

How could I actually explain to him that what he had done was wrong... so wrong... so very wrong... How could I get him to see, to understand?

I stood, faced him, started to speak, but that smug smile of his was back—and I couldn't help myself. I opened my mouth and started... not yelling, but speaking as forcefully as I felt I could without having the entire household hear us.

"You cannot keep playing with people's lives like this! You have to realize at some point just how wrong it is." He started to speak, but I held up a hand, smacked it against his chest. Hard. And kept going. "No! You have to stop it! And you have to go! Now!"

He stepped back then. There was hurt in his eyes —and it had nothing to do with the smack of my hand. It was deeper than that. He was right. I hadn't given in on anything. I'd had my choices taken away from me, but I had not given in, not on a single thing. What he didn't understand was how he had done to me precisely what my ex-husband had done... so many times.

He had taken away all of my options — and done what he wanted — and, not just to me, but to my sweet babies.

I had found a way to recover the memories he'd stolen from me, but that had been exceptional circumstances. Would the children be able to do the same thing? Could they? Was there anything strong enough to compel them to remember?

Did I really want them to?

"I do not understand."

"I know. You don't. And, that's a big part of the problem. I don't even know if you can. How could you? In the same way I can never be the same as I was, you can't change who you've always been. You're not human. You never will be. And, thanks to you, I never can be again. And there's nothing either of us can do to change that."

He stood there, looking at me. Looking right through me. I didn't have to read his mind to feel the confusion. It was all over his face. But, I no longer cared to help him solve it.

"You really need to go." I turned my back then. Closing him out of my mind so easily now, it was almost like turning off a light switch.

Thanks to all of the new knowledge that had flooded my brain, and then slowly unpacked itself, showing me exactly what I needed to do to control my new abilities, I knew exactly how to block him out. How to close myself off from him. I couldn't hear his thoughts and he couldn't access mine. He couldn't charm me. And he couldn't take my memories anymore.

If only I had figured it out just a little faster. The thought brought tears to my eyes—and, at the same time, I heard the familiar swoosh of water as he made his exit.

When he was gone, I held on for almost ten full seconds.

I stood straight and strong, reminding myself that he had done bad things. From the first moment I had met him, he'd been manipulating me. He had taken my humanity. He had tried to steal my memories. He had turned me into a freak who would eventually have to leave my family—for their own safety. He had robbed my sweet babies of the only good memories they had... would ever have... of their father.

And he had assured that their father would never make any memories with them... ever again.

And he saw nothing wrong with any of it. He'd actually seemed oddly proud of it. Like he had done something so fantastic, so magnanimous, I should be thanking him.

I didn't notice the tears at first. I didn't hear the rain outside. I only felt the pain inside of me—as if I was being torn into two pieces, two jagged, broken, messy pieces that could never be put back together again in quite the same way.

And then I was on my knees, sinking to the floor, doing everything I could to quiet the sobs that threatened to actually tear me in two.

Arms came around me. Not his, but arms that were familiar anyway. They wrapped around me and held on tight, but I couldn't seem to stop crying. I couldn't get the wracking sobs to stop. I reached for darkness, prayed for it, welcomed it. And only those arms around me—and the knowledge that they could not follow where I wanted so desperately to go—kept me anchored to where I was.

However, darkness... of a different sort did come. As I wore myself out, my body gave way to exhaustion and I fell into such a deep sleep, I didn't even dream.

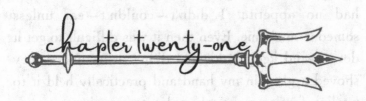

TIME PASSED SO SLOWLY I LOST COUNT of the days. Putting one foot in front of the other, somehow I managed to drag myself out of bed each morning, go to the job that paid our mortgage. The house was one of those things I had convinced myself was worth whatever I had to do to keep it, even if it meant continuing to work at the most boring job I'd ever had.

My job made me miserable. If I thought about it, it didn't make sense. I used to love my job. I used to get along with my co-workers. I used to look forward to going to work. Not anymore.

There was no joy at work... or at home, either. Which troubled me, because I had always loved being at home with my children and my mother. I had never needed to go out partying or anything to find joy. Being at home had always brought me tremendous joy... laughter... love. Not anymore. I was miserable.

My mother brought me all my favorite foods, but I had no appetite. I didn't—couldn't—eat unless someone made me. Even then it was difficult to get it down—and keep it down. I didn't drink unless they shoved a glass in my hand and practically held it to my lips, forcing me to take at least a few sips.

I existed... only just.

Losing him, I lost myself, too. How was I to know that pushing him out of my life was pushing away my will to survive. I detested what I was doing to my family, but I was barely holding on to life.

Nothing that could have happened before could have prepared me for how broken I would feel, cutting myself off from the man I'd never wanted to be connected to in the first place.

How much time passed, I couldn't say... would likely never really know. I continued to exist—and only exist. I was a zombie, wandering through the days and nights.

Empty, broken, stripped bare, no more than a hollow shell.

"All right. That is enough."

My mother's words barely registered with me. It was the shaking that finally did it.

Even then, it was a full ten seconds before I realized someone was speaking to me, holding my arms and shaking me as if trying to wake me.

"What?"

"Enough is enough. Call him... or whatever it is that you do. You can't..." She spread her arms out on either side, before she dropped them and went on. "We can't go on like this, Kelsey. So, enough already."

"I can't."

"You can't what?" Her voice was no longer just annoyed. There was something more—there was anger.

"Mom, I can't call him."

"Why not." There was frustration now, too.

"I shut him out. I closed myself off from him. He can't hear me anymore. Besides..."

"Besides, what?" Clearly, this conversation was not going the way she'd envisioned, the way she'd wanted it to go when she'd started shaking me.

"He wouldn't want to hear from me anyway."

"That is bullsh... I'm sorry, but that's nonsense."

I said nothing. There was nothing to say.

There was a full ten seconds of silence, before the shouting started.

"This is beyond ridiculous! That man... Yes, I know he's not just a man, but he wanted to be with you so badly, he came here to try and convince you of it. He was clearly in love with you. I don't pretend to understand everything about him, but even I could see that. A blind man could have seen it! He wants to hear from you!" Then, a second later. "Believe me! He definitely wants to hear from you!"

I just sat there. I couldn't think of anything to say —and I knew I could never convince her of what had been right in front of me, but I also knew he hadn't put up a fight when I blocked him out.

He'd just left.

He'd run away. And he hadn't come back. He hadn't tried to communicate with me. There were no notes, no messengers, no mysterious deliveries, no dreams or wayward thoughts pushed into my head.

Nothing.

But how could I explain that to my mother? She'd never known the full extent of how we had communicated, how connected we had been. How could she possibly understand how the absolute lack of connection was slowly killing me?

"Please, sweetheart? Find a way to call him—or just go to him. You can't go on like this. You're not even half living. You're an empty shell of a person.

We want you back, even if it means we have to share you with him." She sounded nearly broken now. Tears flowed down her cheeks. No longer angry or annoyed, just broken.

After a few seconds, she added a very quiet. "Please."

I hesitated. After spending so much energy shutting him out, I honestly didn't know if I did call him, whether or not he would answer. Or come at my call. And did I really want to? After what he had done?

"Stop that." Her voice was annoyed again, which was better than broken, but still... unexpected.

"You're trying to talk yourself out of it. I see it in your face."

"I'm not."

"Yes, you are. Don't lie to your mother." She wagged a finger toward my face.

I hadn't told her what he'd done. Would she even believe me? Especially if she no longer remembered Neal as well. Would she think I was crazy? Would she be as angry as I had been—side with me in choosing not to call him?

I almost didn't want to say anything... I didn't want to admit it, but I really did want to call him, go to him, anything to get him back. I just didn't know if I had the courage to try.

"Just what is stopping you, young lady?"

"If you knew what he did..." I couldn't finish the

thought. If I explained... whether she believed me or not, she would likely be as angry as I had been.

"Kelsey, tell me!" It wasn't a question. It was more of a demand. She was leaving me no choice. I knew she wasn't going to take no for an answer now.

For the first time, I looked up at her, really looked at her. "He took away the children's memories of their father."

She looked at me for a full ten seconds, her face completely unreadable in that time. Then she blinked. "And?"

"And what? He took away all the memories they had of their father. Good. Bad. Everything in between. Took them away. And they'll never get them back. They're just gone. Forever." I couldn't tell if she believed me or not. Did she even remember Neal—and she thought I was crazy? Or making it up? Even worse, did she not remember him—and still thought I was crazy?

I seriously couldn't tell.

"Look, I know you've been a member of the walking dead around here for the last few weeks, but you have to have noticed the change in both kids... at least a little."

Now it was my turn to blink. I shook my head a little as I tried to figure out what she was trying to say.

"I guess you haven't." She sounded disappointed now. In me.

I wanted to apologize. I actually opened my mouth to do so before I realized that if I was "an empty shell" the past few weeks, then how would I have noticed a change in the kids. I realized that I hadn't noticed anything going on around me since he had left.

"No. I haven't noticed. I've been a little preoccupied."

"Yes. You have. You've been walking around here in a daze, ignoring your children, ignoring your life, ignoring me. Why exactly did you fight so hard to come back here to us if you were just going to ignore us all?"

I couldn't say anything to defend myself, because it was true. Mother was completely and totally right. I had been ignoring everyone. I might as well have been under the ocean a thousand miles away for all the attention I had paid to the life around me for weeks...

Did she really say weeks? It's been weeks?

"*Yes, my love. It has.*"

With those five words, he did what I hadn't had the courage to do. He restored the connection between us. I finally felt fully alive again. Feeling rushed through me again at the touch of his mind. Colors were vibrant again. So much so, it was a little overwhelming. I hadn't even realized the whole world had looked almost grey until the color was back again.

Where. Have. You. Been?

Why were you not speaking to me? Why did you just go away and leave me all alone?

"It was what you wished."

Really? You left, severed our connection, stayed away, let me walk around here like a shell of a person for weeks —because you thought it was what I wished?

"I did not sever our connection."

His words were unexpected. But he was right. He did not sever our connection. I had done that. I had knowingly and willfully severed our connection. And I knew it. I remembered the moment I had figured out how—and I'd done it, without a second thought.

"You were very angry." He sounded sad now. Regretful.

He truly sounded like he regretted something... his part on the memory erasure—maybe.

"I know you were angry when you learned what I did, but I truly did believe it was the right thing to do. Your daughter suffered so over the indifference of that man."

He didn't even use Neal's name. I did notice that. Of course he heard my thought...

"I will not. He does not deserve to be named by such a person as me." There was the arrogant Sea King I knew so well.

I'm sure you're right. I didn't argue, but I did my best to tuck away my amusement at his tone and his superiority. It was a little humorous.

"I am not humorous. I do not exist to amuse you." His tone was imperious again.

Are you sure about that? Maybe you can't help that

you do. You probably don't even mean to. Oh. How I'd missed this.

"I know. I've missed it, too."

Oh shush.

"You know how to make me shush."

The images he put in my mind then were more than a little embarrassing... sitting in the kitchen with my mother watching me — with a look that told me she knew more than she should about what I was doing at the moment.

"What?"

"You're doing it, aren't you?"

I tried to look innocent. I really tried. "Doing what?"

"Talking to him."

I tried to maintain the facade. But, I could see it was no use. She had figured it out. How, I had no idea. I didn't even try to pretend. I had to know. "How did you know?"

"I've seen you do this a lot. Not lately. But... ever since you brought him home, until a few weeks ago, you did it a lot — and he tended to show up just after. Or else, you did it when he was here, when neither of you were talking to us."

"But how did you know?"

"I didn't know. I guessed. I'm right though, aren't I?" She was definitely too smart.

"Yeah. Good guess." Had we been that obvious?

"I do believe you underestimate her as well as

yourself." He sounded entirely too smug. But he was right. I had never given myself credit for anything. It was easier putting myself down.

"I could come to you. Make you see what an incredible person you are. Would you believe it then?"

Part of me wanted to say yes, come to me. My heart leapt at the chance to see him. But another part of me wanted to say no—to keep my distance until I figured out what I really wanted from all of this.

"I think you know what it is you want." After only a moment, he added, *"Or who it is you want."*

I stopped myself before the snarky comment I was almost thinking became a comment he could hear. I knew he was right, but he had no idea how hard it was for me to admit it. And I had obviously hurt him as much as I had hurt myself with this separation. I needed to be sure this time—before committing myself to him. I had the feeling when I did, it would be forever.

My attention was yanked away from my thoughts by my Mother's shout.

"I knew it!"

I turned just in time to see the water fall away and disappear before Nicholas swept into a low bow right there beside me, aimed in my mother's direction.

How did he...? I didn't get the chance to verbalize it or finish the thought. He was already kissing me with a burning desire I couldn't ignore—I could only take what he was offering. He always knew what I was thinking before I seemed to—and he was answering the thought I didn't get to think.

"Then you know I don't want to ask you to stop, but I have to. My mother is standing here watching us. Please stop."

Amazingly, he did stop. Then he took a step back.

"It is not only your thoughts I am connected to, you know. Your family truly is as much a part of you as you say."

That thought stopped me cold. Was this why he had been convinced he was doing the right thing by erasing Neal from the children's minds? Because he had looked into their minds and seen the damage he'd done to them all these years? Maybe even to Dylan? He had always seemed like he enjoyed his father's company—like he looked forward to seeing him, and spending time doing things with him. Was there more to it than that—something I had missed?

How had Nicholas sensed something in my children that I had missed?

"I am the Sea King. I miss nothing."

At that, I laughed out loud.

My mother looked confused, but happy at the same time. Probably because I had laughed. Not ten minutes ago, she had been so worried about me—and now I was laughing. And Nicholas was here. And she didn't see any reason I should let what he had done get in the way of going on with things.

"See. I knew he would come if you called. Didn't I tell you he would?" She sounded so happy with herself, I couldn't bear to tell her that I hadn't called him.

Nicholas could though. "Actually, Celeste, she did not call me."

She looked from him to me and back again, obviously confused. "Then, how...? I don't understand."

Nicholas looked at me before answering her. "Your daughter is quite unmovable when she sets her mind on a course of action."

"Kelsey." There was that voice I had heard as long as I could remember... the mother, disappointed in her child, the child who had done something stupid or stubborn or outright foolish... or all three.

I was sure it fit somehow, but I was not ready to admit that I had been entirely in the wrong over what he had done—and my reaction to it. If I had not sent him away, would he have ever realized that what he'd done might not have been the right way to handle things?

"Celeste..." His voice was quiet, calming, soothing, yet filled with something I had yet to hear from him— humility.

When my mother looked up at him, he went on. "She was not entirely in the wrong. She sent me away because she felt that she must defend her children.

The mother within her—the woman you taught her to be—felt very strongly that I had wronged her children... your grandchildren."

My mother didn't argue. She was actually nodding.

"She was right to do what she did."

At his admission, I gasped in surprise. I hadn't seen, felt or heard that coming. He had kept a tight lock on the thought. I wondered why—especially if he was going to just announce it... in front of my mother.

And then... I knew. He was ashamed of it. His humility was genuine, complete, and uncomfortable. He regretted his actions—truly. However, like what he had done with me initially—changing me without my permission, taking my memories, stealing me from my family... there was no going back from this.

What was done... was done.

There was no going back. We both knew that. It had been very well established that his abilities were permanent, unchangeable.

Which was one of the reasons I had been so angry in the first place.

"It is also the reason I did not give you the answer to your question about your family."

So, you do have an answer.

"I do, yes."

"And..." I was practically holding my breath, waiting.

"I could not bear to tell you. There is no going back. You know this as well as I do now. If only one of them

makes the decision to stay behind, what will you do? How would you handle it? It would tear you apart—much more than our separation has done. You are a mother first. I understand that now. I did not before. You were correct about that."

Then it can be done? They could join us under the sea. It wasn't a question. He had answered me—even if he didn't mean to.

"Yes, my love. But how can you even offer it to them, not knowing what their decision will be? Could you truly leave one of them behind?"

I won't have to. My words might have been premature, but I felt so strongly about it. I was sure I knew what they would decide. At ehe very least, Cassie would jump at the chance. She'd always wanted to be a mermaid. Dylan would be harder. He would not want to lose his video games. He would struggle, but I had to believe that, if given the choice between coming with me... or losing me forever, he would choose his mother, and his sister.

My mother was the only one who was really a mystery. If given the choice, what would she do? Which world would she pick? Would she come with her family, the only family she had left really... or stay behind with everything that was familiar to her.

I didn't have to ask, it turned out.

I looked over to where she had been sitting—but she wasn't there. She stood next to Nicholas, in a wall of water, a half-smile on her face.

"I guess I really should have told you a long time ago, sweetie."

Dive
DEEP
for the
TREASURE
that you
SEEK

~ *Unkown*

TO MY READERS

Hello there, and thank you for reading my book!

I don't know how many other authors write from their dreams, but I do. The first novel that I actually finished was directly from a dream I had—one that has haunted me for years. It hasn't been published yet, but I hope... one day...

This story is also from a dream I had—though it certainly took on a life all its' own as I wrote it down. So, it only very loosely resembles that long ago dream (Which could be one of the reasons it has taken me so very long to get it all down on paper, but who knows...)

Kelsey is not me. She may have started out that way, but she is not now. I'm actually a little happy and also a little sad about that. She has become the person I really want to be. So, I guess that's a goal I can work toward...

Anyway, I hope you enjoy her story as much as I have!

   THANKS for reading!

THANK YOU!

I would love to tell you that this is another one for my readers, but the truth is, this story is all for my sweet Macy—who has always wanted to be a mermaid.

She actually jokes that she must be half mermaid already. She swims like a mermaid WITHOUT the use of a mono-fin. She doesn't seem to feel the cold like anyone else I know and absolutely hates heat. We live in a great place for the first part and the absolute worst place for the second. The south has not only monstrous heat, but where we are, the humidity makes that heat even worse.

Anyway, I do want to thank each and every one of you because you have waited oh so patiently for me to write another novel... for so many years.

Thanks to all of you, I have a reason to write. Thanks to you, I haven't given up. Thanks to you, I have gotten back to work - and I'm going stronger than ever! And I can't wait to share the stories that are still very much a part of me—with all of you!

Blessings to you all!

COMING SOON

NEW FROM JC

chapter one

Have you ever had one of those moments? One when you were absolutely certain you saw someone in the corner of your vision. But you knew it was impossible to have seen anyone — because no one else is there in the house with you!

When you live alone, and you're the type of person who tends to stay up writing late into the night, those moments can be more than a little frightening.

What would you do in that situation?

What would you do if one of those moments happened... and it wasn't even a little frightful? How would you handle it, if it was amazing... fantastic... unbelievable... even life-changing?

I can tell you what I did — not in one, but two cases.

The first time it happened, there was nothing particularly spectacular about it...

I shrugged my shoulders, took a deep breath, and dove back into the story that had kept me from sleep for so many days that I had finally lost count.

It was the latest in a long line of stories that had whispered to me urgently, keeping me distracted, until I worked feverishly to record every single bit of it.

Writing was much more than a passion for me. I had spent most of my life pursuing it... much like a starving man searches for his next meal.

First, moving across the country to attend college. I eagerly plunged into my classes, studying literature and creative writing in all its forms, as well as a few other courses that piqued my interest. I focused mostly on classes that would enhance my writing.

I didn't bother to take physical fitness courses, since I waited tables until the early hours. Sometimes as much as seven nights a week.

I had found a tiny apartment to share with friends. And I continued to save every penny, carving out time to write when I should have been sleeping and turning down invitations from friends to party or socialize.

Whether or not exhaustion consumed my body when I stumbled in from work, the words came before everything else, including food, sleep, even chatting with my roommates.

After a quick shower, I would start a pot of coffee, pour a cup... and usually forget to drink it because I had lost myself in my writing. Eventually I would reheat it in the microwave, then I would promptly forget it again under the harsh taskmaster that was my own imagination.

And so it was, when I found myself aware of a presence occupying the same space as I, by way of a tell-tale shadow hovering at the corner of my vision during a time when I knew not one of my room-mates was at home. I stopped, sat straight up, and turned my head to where the person should have been.

Of course, there was nothing and no one there. No roommate creeping in to watch me work. No apparition or ghostly figure there to haunt me. No tell-tale shadow.

Whether or not it had been real or my imagination was the only question... one that had never truly been answered.

With no answers, and no hope of any, I had dived back into my writing, pushing the odd occurrence to the same corner of my mind where I held my own personal theories about fantasy, science fiction, and all of the beloved stories that had kept me company while growing up.

Nothing like that happened again. Not for many years. When it did happen again, I was writing in much the same circumstances, in the early hours of morning, as had become my habit.

I was alone in the house, this time due to a lack of roommates. I was again in the middle of a sentence. And ironically enough, I was working within the same story world.

Having sold my first story... one within what had been my favorite fantasy world for — at the time — a large sum, with no agreement for royalties or further earnings, and with no expectation of being allowed to write any sequels, I should have, by all rights, let the the story go.

But for some unexplainable reason I had never been able to. It had not been the first story I'd ever written, but there had always been something about it which had kept hold of me.

The characters and their world had stayed with me, so vividly that I'd written enough material to fill at least three full-length novels in the years since. This was in spite of three books from a completely different series that I had written and which had been published since.

So once again, I found myself sitting straight up in my chair, stretching muscles and bones too long cramped into the typical writer's hunch, and looking over at the deep armchair that rested beside the wide bay window that I loved so much, it had all but sold the house... a blessing for the harried, frustrated realtor who had shown me at least three dozen houses before this one.

In that favorite, overstuffed armchair, which I found such a wonderful place to curl up with a favorite novel the few times I tore myself away from my own writing, sat a man... a slightly strange looking man.

His eyes were too large for his face. His mouth had an oddly stretched look to it. His fingers were decidedly too long. His posture was much too still. And he looked at me in a way that felt more like he were looking through me, right into my head... my thoughts... or even beyond.

Though there was not one thing about the man, who was most certainly not human, that frightened or even startled me. His presence gave the impression of such respect and awe, that I could not help but feel as I did at one of the many events I had attended over the years.

These were events where I was asked to speak to readers, as well as to sign books, both from the beloved series that was well beyond my control and the unrelated ones that had, nevertheless, done exceptionally well all on their own.

Whenever I looked out on the crowds of people waiting to hear me speak, or standing in line with books clutched lovingly to their chests, or opened as they began to read—unable to wait even for the coveted signature before diving in, I felt the same sort of expectation that was flowing from the unearthly man calmly sitting in my favorite chair.

And in that moment, I knew... I absolutely knew... that whatever he was doing here, he meant me no harm.

Of course I had no way of knowing what he was doing here in my home, in a world that was clearly not his own. I would have thought I was dreaming, but for the pain in my neck from having it turned so far to look at him. For what was now turning into a very large amount of time.

With the pain demanding much of my attention, I determined to do something about it before trying to attempt an inquiry of this visitor. With deliberately slow movements, I unfolded the legs that were nearly asleep at any rate, and settled them to the floor in front of my computer chair.

Then I gently pushed against the wood until my chair began to roll backward, giving myself just enough room to allow the passage of my knees around the sides of the opening under my desk.

I nearly cringed as the wheels on the chair squeaked, but the man made no move, said nothing, did not even blink as my chair continued to roll.

I carefully moved my feet to swivel, turning my head slowly as I did so, determined to keep my eyes trained on the chair on the other side of the room and its occupant, certain that if I were to lose sight of him for even a moment, he would disappear as quickly as he had arrived.

He remained there. Whether it was because I kept my eyes on him or not, it was unclear. After several long moments, he finally moved, shifting forward so quickly, the movement itself was a blur. But there was nothing frightening in the movement.

On the contrary, I was fascinated, even if a bit confused at first. One moment he was sitting stiff and straight, and in the next moment he had shifted so that he perched on the edge of the large chair.

And still he said nothing.

I waited. Part of me wanted to speak, but again, I was hesitant that he would disappear if I spoke. I also felt there was a distinct possibility he did not speak my language. Though, why would he be here if he could not speak to me?

Seconds dragged out as I waited... stretched out until each one felt more like a year than a moment. I took the opportunity to look more closely at the strange being perched delicately on my chair.

His strange eyes were not only too large, they were inexplicably dark. There was no white area to be seen... just a grayish black that seemed to move and shift like the fog it so closely resembled.

It was impossible, no matter how I tried from this distance, to tell if his mouth was actually made up of two lips or not. There was a definite shape to the area of his face where humans had lips, but since he had barely moved—and had not yet spoken, there was no way to tell if it was actually his mouth, and whether that mouth was made up of lips or of something else.

His fingers, one of which had, at the moment I happened to look down at it, suddenly and inexplicably began tapping the arm of the chair where it rested in a complex sort of pattern.

There was no sound, just a constant movement that could have been anything... from the beat of a song that was stuck in his head... to some complex form of morse code that I could never hope to decipher.

I had but a moment to think what a disaster this would all turn out to be if that were the case, before he opened that strange mouth and spoke. And when he did, his voice so mesmerized me, that I very nearly missed the actual words he was speaking.

In fact, he may have actually repeated himself without my having noticed, so entranced was I by the sound of his other-worldly voice.

"We are in desperate need of your help." were the words I heard.

However, there was a distinct separation of sounds. What I heard spoken aloud was decidedly not English. But those words—while clearly English—sounded as well, whether aloud or in my head, I could not tell.

Several long seconds passed again as I sat there, thinking about the sounds I'd heard, the entrancing sound of his voice, and the shape of his strange mouth as it formed the words.

Even as he was speaking unintelligible words, I marveled over the two distinct sets of words spoken and heard... or perhaps one spoken and one somehow magically translated only inside my head.

And then those strange lips widened in the most breathtaking smile I ever remember seeing in my life. Nearly terrible in its perfection, the smile lit up his entire face, making it almost painful to look at. I finally did look away... almost not caring whether he disappeared, yet at the same time terrified he would be gone when... if... I dared to look back.

Thankfully he did not disappear. After what felt like an eternity, I did look back. He was still in exactly the same position he'd been in, perched on the edge of my chair, no longer smiling now, but wearing an expression that was—for the first time—nearly frightening.

Before I could take it in that indeed I should be frightened, I heard the strange double layer of speech again, but this time with a compelling urgency that I seemed to actually feel deep within me as he spoke.

"Time is of the essence."

I managed to respond. "What does that mean, exactly? And how could I possibly help you? For that matter, who are you?"

"We are the link. We bring inspiration. We bridge the gap between worlds." He hesitated for a moment, while watching me. Perhaps to give me time to digest what had been said.

None of it really answered my questions, but clearly it was meant to do so. I nodded, but said nothing. Fortunately, he went on.

"Your world is unique in the vast cosmos we all inhabit. You wield a particular sort of magic, a tremendous force that fuels those in need." And once again, he waited.

I closed my eyes for a moment, taking time to think about what he had said. Had this strange visitor actually just told me that our world had magic... real magic?

Somehow I knew he didn't mean the type of magic

one could see at an act in Vegas.

Was this supposed to be the way he wanted me to help them? Did he think I had magic? And that it was extremely powerful?

As I continued to try and make sense of his words — and the meaning behind them — he spoke again.

"You do not understand. This is expected." There was a tiny nod of his head, and then he kept going. "This is not the way our interaction is meant to be. Your people were never meant to know that we exist. We were to stay hidden, acting as your muse, providing inspiration only. This is the way of things." He stopped again, looking somewhat expectant.

And then, somehow, suddenly I was reminded again of that strange early morning so many long years ago, when I had been so certain someone was in the room with me. Only, when I had turned that morning to look, there had been no one in sight.

Had he been here then, too? Sitting in the same sort of place, because I'd had a chair in roughly the same place in my tiny room in that cramped apartment. A chair for the same purpose. A quiet place by the window where I could sit and read.

That time, when I had felt the hairs on the back of my neck stand up, feeling certain someone else was in the room with me — even though I had known it was impossible — I had looked for someone.

Had he momentarily forgotten to hide himself then? Or had he nearly shown himself for some other reason, only to change his mind and remain hidden before I had actually seen him?

He was nodding again in short, quick, blurred movements.

"You are correct."

That was it. Nothing else. No clues as to which part of the whole thing I was right about... which had me wondering if he could read my mind... or not?

He did not answer that question. He said nothing else, but continued to watch me for the moment. After several long seconds, I gathered up the courage to speak, voicing the question he hadn't answered, almost hoping he would answer with a yes — and at the same time, not really sure I wanted to know.

"Can you read my mind."

Before I had even finished asking, he was shaking his head. "We do not interfere in that way. We would not. We are only meant to inspire. We do not invade."

I realized, even as the words translated themselves somehow, he was still only half answering my query.

Was he trying to answer, but was unable to accurately address every little bit, or was he deliberately answering only the part I must know? There was really no way of knowing, so it would have to do.

And now I felt certain that getting any answers would be much more difficult. Clearly there was some sort of language barrier here, even if it was only that his language did not seem to translate precisely into English.

I would have to be very careful — and very precise — if I hoped to understand the slightest idea of what exactly it was he thought I could do to help him... or them... or whatever.

Direct approach then... "All right. So, what exactly is it you need from me?"

He did not speak. He simply closed those large, strange eyes. A moment later, I pushed backward into my chair, nearly knocking it over.

Images were filling my head. Scenes I was familiar with. Scenes I had thought of all too often as I sat in my chair, writing — and wishing — that I could somehow visit the place I saw in my imagination.

There was the spectacular silver city I had written so much about. The waterfalls that thundered behind it were just as majestic as I had always imagined them.

The sweeping green and blue fields that spread out on either side until meeting up with the dozens of industrial little villages that dotted the countryside around what I had always thought of as the capital city. The towering trees that sheltered those villages, and served as a comforting, familiar background.

There were people everywhere. A small group of children were running across the fields, trailing some kite-like sort of contraption. Several adults pushed heavily laden carts up the wide street that led to the main gates of the city. Others were tiny specks as they worked the distant fields of some blue-colored plant that I figured must be their version of wheat.

The clear, deep purple sky was dotted with fluffy silver clouds... comforting, reassuring, constant, cheerful.

It was the place of my dreams—of my fantasies.

MORE FROM JC

WRITTEN WITH
MACY MORROWS

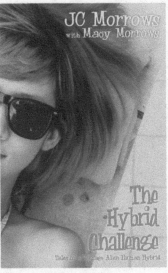

ABOUT THE AUTHOR

JC Morrows, author of the **Order of the MoonStone** YA Dystopian series — including Best Seller *A Reluctant Assassin*, and the action packed **Frozen World** series; a Post-Apocalyptic series with a Dystopian edge — spends her days writing, reading, juggling two kids, and wishing someone would invent a coffee IV. A storyteller in the truest sense of the word, JC has been telling stories in one form or another her entire life and once her mother convinced her to write them down, she simply couldn't stop.

FOLLOW JC ON SOCIAL MEDIA

FACEBOOK

INSTAGRAM

WEB

GOODREADS

ABOUT THE PUBLISHER

here at
Mystic Moonstone Press
actively seek out fun and fantastical
stories that every member of the family
can read and enjoy!

We hope you will check out our works and
join us on our journey!

Printed in the USA
CPSIA information can be obtained
at www.ICGtesting.com
CBHW011454261024
16475CB00022B/1853